Pirates, Gamblers
And
Scalawags

Pirates, Gamblers and Scalawags

Tales of Fernandina Characters

And Other Stories

David Tuttle

Library of Congress Control Number: 2007922200
Tuttle, David 1941 –
Pirates, Gamblers, and Scalawags

ISBN: 978-0-9677419-5-6

Published by Lexington Ventures, Inc.
1894 So. 14th Street
Fernandina Beach, FL 32034

Printed in the United States of America

Cover Design by Thomas R. Johannes
Illustrations by William R. Maurer

Other publications by David Tuttle:
Murder in Fernandina
The Leopard of Fernandina

Contents

Dedicated to those spirits that still
walk along Centre Street.

Acknowledgements

Writing a piece that people want to read is not as simple as might be thought. For me, I need to hear, "good" or "bad" from my first reader, my wife Barbara.

After working and reworking a piece, my editor, Emily Carmain, takes me to task. Emily knows what I'm trying to say and guides me safely through the minefield.

My publisher, Don Shaw, always gently nudges me along and for this I'm grateful. Certainly in getting a book from the author to the reader, many people play a role. Jan Johannes and his son, Thomas, do wonders in formatting and cover designs. Their skill is extremely valuable. A special thank you to William Maurer who has illustrated this work with his special artistic skills. Thanks Bill.

Thanks to you, the reader, who asked for more after reading Murder In Fernandina and The Leopard of Fernandina. The third Lt. Wilson Mystery is nearing completion. In the meantime, enjoy reading about a few of Fernandina's other characters

The Ghost Ship

Juan Carlo de Silva, navigator and first mate, stood on the deck of the *Esperanza* with his dark eyes toward the inlet, beyond which lay the Spanish settlement on Amelia Island. The small garrison of Spanish soldiers at Amelia Island Post was waiting to greet them, due in part to the arrival of fresh supplies from their home far across the Atlantic. Several ships followed them on the incoming tide, sails full from the offshore wind.

The cruel Captain Santos and Juan hoped none of the crew would run away during this short layover. Juan had seen Captain Santos have men flogged for the simplest infraction of the stern rules he'd set down. He treated his officers with restrained respect, but the crew was no more to him than the stray dogs that ran along the wharves. But Juan knew they wouldn't be able to run far on the island. The few natives that were here would be able to find any missing crew member quickly and return him for a reward.

The cold ocean water ran through Captain Santos' veins. His father and two brothers had been at sea when they lost their lives. Fear drove Captain Santos to be cold and harsh with his crew. Rarely did a crewman ever sign up for a second voyage with him. Juan had been with Captain Santos for two voyages and this, the third, was going to be Juan's last. He was ready to have his own ship, given to him by a consortium of bankers in Spain. The gold flowing out of Central and South America was continuing to build up the coffers of the Spanish treasury. Bankers were taking their cut off the top and giving the rest to the monarchy. A deal that few knew about.

English and French pirates made the voyages dangerous despite the rich rewards to the ship captains that sailed in to Spanish ports with their golden treasures. This new ship, a three-masted bark, was one of the fastest on the seas. The hull was clean of barnacles and the voyage to Amelia Island was a full day faster than Juan had seen.

Once inside the inlet, the *Esperanza* made the port turn and furled many sails, leaving only those that would help in bringing it to anchorage at Egan's Creek to gently lie against Zephaniah Kingsley's pier. Juan stood alongside Captain Santos on the foredeck. The captain signaled aft to the helmsman with the wave of a raised hand. Within minutes the ship nudged the wooden pilings and made fast with sturdy hawsers.

A shout went up from the men, only to be silenced by the burning glare from the captain. They were happy to be in port again, where the main order of business was trade and providing a military presence -- and, of course, wherever the Spanish settled, there was a mission for the Church.

The captain stood blocking the gangplank. Lines were lowered to the deck from the cranes on shore. The ship also carried supplies to a port in Central America, so only a few barrels of wine, flour and a meager amount of spices were hauled up and over to shore here. The garrison's commandant ordered men with rifles to guard the shipment against thievery. Juan was still on the foredeck as the unloading operation was carried out. He toyed with the idea of going ashore later in the day.

Captain Santos was eager to set sail again but the ship, too, needed supplies of fresh water and fresh meat. They bought fresh vegetables from an English woman named Maria Fernandez. She was becoming known as the vegetable chandler for the island's visiting ships. Fresh supplies were critical on the sea. On longer voyages, where rations began to rot, the cook would add hot spices to cover the foul taste. Often men would get sick and on occasion die of dysentery and be tossed overboard. When there was an outbreak of illness aboard, the cook would stop the practice of "spicing up" the rations.

Kingsley's pier sang out with a mixture of languages due to the varied backgrounds of the workers. The Spanish were eager to populate the island, thus welcomed anyone willing to move here. Consequently, some Englishmen had stayed behind when England left Florida to the Spanish. Black men from Africa, some free, some slaves, some escaped slaves, spoke different dialects to each other amid the cursing and din of unloading and loading the cargo. Warehouses dotted the landscape.

Nearly one hundred ships, flying flags from Germany, Denmark, Norway and even Russia, bobbed in the natural harbor. With the United States only a few hundred yards to the north, smuggling was a thriving business. The political turmoil of embargoes caused smugglers to risk certain death if caught by United States officials. They rowed small skiffs loaded with coffee, tea, sugar, and spirited drink over to the port of St. Mary's in Georgia, then returned with apples, corn, tobacco and rice to the waiting ships heading for European ports.

Riding the next early morning tide, the river pilot guided the *Esperanza* past the inlet, and once in deep water, the ship raised all sails. Only one man failed to return to the ship and it was rumored by the Indians that a white man tried to swim across the river to the marshy land on the other side. They didn't report if he made it or not, only that he was having trouble with the currents.

Juan had stayed aboard and plotted the course south along the coast of Florida, bypassing the large town of St. Augustine. Careless talk aboard the ship indicated a merchant in St. Augustine wanted to find the captain. Something to do with a merchant's daughter.

At six feet tall, the stature and dark complexion of Juan Carlo de Silva, who stood over all the men on the ship, bespoke a Moorish heritage. Often the captain would make derisive remarks about his height, but Juan would only smile. His eyes would search the faces of those who spoke to him and he listened with intensity. The captain questioned him once about the ritual of trimming his neat beard every two days, even at sea. His response was that it made him feel clean; he did not like untidiness. The boyish handsome face did not reveal that he was twenty-five and a veteran at sea.

The captain was the antithesis in his appearance. His five feet four inches height belied the fact that he would fight any man that crossed him, and he had a scarred face to prove it. His temper was legendary among the Spanish sailors. Juan witnessed him sending a man overboard to be towed behind the ship for an hour for arguing with the ship's cook. The captain's thick black hair and beard were never kept in line, especially at sea. The slight figure contrasted with the booming deep voice that could be heard over the fiercest gale. His only redeeming asset was he had never lost a ship or cargo.

Juan and Santos had respect for each other but only spoke to each other when necessity arose. At sea, each man was his own company. Sea captains were normally their own navigators, but the company wanted Captain Santos to have a navigator on board the *Esperanza*. Santos didn't like the idea and expressed his disappointment, to no avail.

The *Esperanza* sailed into the Atlantic and turned starboard aiming down the coast, staying landward of the Gulf Stream, so as to not buck the northbound current. Juan would stand on the foredeck for hours to watch the sea unfold before him, as he did this day.

When they had reached the southern tip of Florida, Juan altered course southeast to cut diagonally across the Gulf Stream. They passed Cuba's eastern coast, then on toward Colon at the isthmus of Central America. Built for speed and hauling a cargo of gold, the ship had few cannon aboard, the thought being that it could outrun any pirates.

The wind was in their favor on the night of September 20, 1812. They were well into the Gulf of Mexico. The low swells gave hint that the calms might strike the next day. Until then the winds had been to their back the whole voyage. As first mate, Juan had the evening watch and before turning the helm over to the second mate, he sent a man aloft to check rigging. Juan watched the man scamper among the lines, stop while looking aft, then climb higher.

The sailor called down that he spied a light aft of the ship. Juan and the helmsman thought he was referring to the luminescence of the wake. But the crewman said the lights were from a ship. Juan stood for several minutes as the *Esperanza* rolled in the swells. He would glimpse the lights and then they would disappear. They were like none he'd seen before, not from another ship or a town's lights reflecting off low clouds. The helmsman made the sign of the cross and wanted to go get the captain, but Juan said the captain could do nothing. After watching for another twenty minutes, Juan sent a second man aloft. This time the man said the lights were steady, meaning the ship had gained on them. By then, Juan could plainly see the lights in the distance.

The captain was sent for and came topside growling. He cuffed the cabin boy standing nearby. Juan relayed the events that had passed and Captain Santos watched the light for a few minutes, and then in the dim lamplight turned to Juan. He muttered a curse and went down to his cabin. The lights following them stayed the same distance while Juan strained his eyes to see a ship, but all he could see were the lights, he counted three of them.

Leaving the watch to the second mate, Juan went below to his tiny cabin, in hopes of getting rest. The mystery of lights appearing from nowhere made it difficult to get to sleep. He didn't remember falling asleep but near dawn a crewman shook him awake, saying the lights had moved closer.

On deck, the helmsman said the lights followed them tack for tack. Juan started to send for the captain, but thought better of it. The ship posed no danger that could be seen. Juan stood for fifteen minutes watching the lights when the winds picked up and the swells grew larger, causing the ship to heave to and fro. The lights would be in view when on the crest of a wave but disappear when in the trough. Shortly the lights were gone altogether. Juan returned to his cabin.

The next day the word got around that a ghost ship was following them, and cruel jokes were told that it was coming for the captain. The winds stayed up enough to fill the sails, giving the crew work to keep them occupied. The captain often ordered course changes, which required men going aloft and setting different lines. The men were getting worn out with the seemingly unnecessary tacks.

Captain Santos was edgy all day, pacing the helm area and looking aft. The sky was bright and sun shone clear, reflecting like little diamonds off the blue-green waters of the Gulf. That night was to be the turning point of the voyage.

Juan was on watch, standing next to the helm. He would occasionally look aft, wondering if the curiosity of the mysterious lights was being felt across his ship. He was uneasy, going down to the deck and checking lines and the trim of the sails. All was going well as the men off duty grabbed a few minutes of precious sleep. The entire crew had toiled under the daytime sun.

In the evening, Juan was forward, watching the stars that rose from the horizon; bright Sirius, the Dog Star, rose to chase Orion across the heavens. The moon wasn't due up for another two hours, ceding to the night an encompassing blackness, almost an enveloping blanket to swallow Juan, were it not for the stars. He looked at the red Betelgeuse and wondered why stars were different colors. On nights like this he felt warmth in his soul and would have felt so this night, save for the nagging intuition that the strange lights were not going away. He mentally waved good night to the stars and went below to his bunk.

He was jolted from his reverie by the hail from the helmsman. The lights were aft again. Juan ran past the helm and leaned against the rail. This time they were closer. Juan ordered a course change and the bell sounded as orders were shouted. Men sprang to life, sprinting aloft to reset the sails. Muttering curses, the men ran up the rigging to the spars.

Juan watched the wake of the *Esperanza* make a slow arc across the water following the new course. In the awakening morning, the ship behind them made the same course change. The rising sun's glow spilled over the horizon to point to a cloudless sky. The wind eased a little and the *Esperanza* slowed, as did the phantom ship. Its masts could be seen now, and it was a brigantine with both masts set to full sail.

Men waking from the night's sleep took turns coming to the rails to see for themselves. Captain Santos was stirred by all the commotion and could be heard bellowing curses as he made his way to the deck. As Santos stared grimly at the following ship, Juan gave him a report of events. Santos wanted to know their position and how long it would be before they made Colon. Juan retrieved his antiquated navigation instruments and hastily made his position report, five days from Colon if the wind held. Santos didn't say a word and went below for his breakfast. He stayed there the whole morning and it was up to Juan to make sure the day's schedule was carried out.

For two days the brigantine followed them, not gaining or lagging behind. The brig was a bit smaller than the *Esperanza* and looked as though it might be faster, yet it stayed the same distance, no matter what sails were aloft. Santos tried to communicate twice by firing the cannon, but got no reply. The men grew more restless; scuffles broke out and were dealt with immediately by Juan, lest the captain have men receive lashes and be washed down with salt water.

A day and a half from Colon, Juan was awakened by the men crying out to Captain Santos to come to the deck. Juan jumped up and was on deck in a flash. Topside there was a great deal of shouting and pushing as the men jostled for a place at the rail. Santos shoved men aside until he too reached the rail. Behind them was the brig, slowly gaining, although there was no wind. It was being propelled by an unseen force. The sails billowed as though full of wind, yet the bow wake was small. Santos ordered the men back to their places or he'd toss a few overboard for shark food.

Juan and Captain Santos stood at the stern rail for half an hour, and by then they gauged the brig to be two miles aft. The captain ordered the four cannon to be loaded, and a round from each cannon was fired, seeking communications. Making the sign of the cross, Juan drew a look of derision from Santos. Juan did not understand how the brig could move in dead air. After the last cannon fired, the brig slowed and its sails went limp, keeping stationary at the same distance.

All hands looked aft. No one had paid attention to the fog that crept over the bow to engulf them. Timber by timber it wrapped itself around them as if it were a big mouth, deliberately swallowing them and taking them down into its gullet to torment them with a slow death by the inner juices of an unseen monster. They were normal men when they began the voyage, not believing in sea monsters or demons of the deep, but now every man on board began to have fears, fears that they hid down deep

in the soul. Those fears no one talks about but put out of
mind lest they creep out at night and drive one insane.

The men began to talk and there were shouts among
them. Some even tried to make the sign of the cross, but
were clumsy since most had never set foot in a church or
at least not since childhood.

An unnatural silence settled in with the fog. The
footfalls of the men on deck were muffled and the air
chilled as the mist grew so thick they could just make
out the outline of the bowsprit. An eerie dampness came
with the gray mist; one that went to the bones, and drops
of water began to form on all surfaces. Men's voices were
barely distinguishable, almost as if they had been removed
from the deck. Voices of those close by were hardest to
hear, yet those on the aft deck could easily hear those
on the bow. Juan spun around from looking at the bow
when he heard the captain gasp and issue a moan.

A dark shadow loomed against the fog to *Esperanza's*
port stern. Ever so slowly the outline and form of the
brigantine appeared. The phantom stopped and lay
nearby. The sails were limp as the ship floated barely a
hundred feet away. The captain took his glass and looked
over the ship as well he could. Juan and Santos strained
to see through the gauzy air but never saw a soul on
deck; not one human was to be seen, no deck hands, no
helmsman...no one. The ships floated, two giant slugs on
a dirty pane of looking-glass.

Juan asked the captain, "What should we do?" The
only response was a whisper that the captain didn't
know.

Santos turned and went down the ladder to his cabin,
never saying a word, but Juan could see in his eyes he was
as afraid as any man on board. When he returned a few

minutes later, Juan could smell the strong whiskey on his breath. Juan didn't blame him. They sat on a coil of line and watched the phantom, talking sporadically in low tones. After several minutes, the captain stood on shaky legs. Saying there was no sense in what was happening, he ordered a dory to be lowered; he was going over to have a look at the visitor.

Juan, the captain and four strong men climbed overboard into a small dory. They each carried a cutlass and the captain had his pistol with him. They set off on the dead calm sea toward the brig. Barely touching the water with the oars, the men rowed in short slow strokes making the trip last as long as they could. The oars made no noise as they dipped into the black water, to keep from offending any evil spirits that might lie ahead.

Juan looked back to his ship and the rails were lined with the men whose eyes were fixed on them, not knowing what to expect and afraid of what might happen next. Suddenly there was a shout from *Esperanza's* deck, and one of the men was pointing to the little dory's starboard side.

Coming out of the fog, the black surface of the water swelled up like a small hill, not cresting but steadily rolling toward them. Shouts of "sea monster" rang out all along the deck. The men were near crazed from the events of the past few days, and now the eerie surroundings didn't lend a hand in bringing sanity.

The sea monster turned out to be a whale, and Juan shouted as much back to the crew. It surfaced between the ships and blew a fine mist into the air. As the men quieted down, Juan drew in a lung full of air and let it out slowly in relief that the black mountain rolling toward them was just a normal sea creature.

The whale's wake rocked the dory and the men quit rowing, hoping to return to their own ship. Santos ordered the men to begin rowing again. Tim Shannon said, "This is foolish. We want to return to our ship."

The captain was a man of short temper and less patience when a man questioned his orders. He raised his pistol and put a ball between Tim's eyes.

Tim fell over into the water, sinking immediately out of sight. Juan saw true fear in the captain's eyes. It was as though he knew what lay ahead and he was fighting it with all his might, knowing all the time that it was he that might not win.

The men began to row while the captain reloaded his pistol. No one saw the swell that approached and built up off the port side. The dory pitched, and the captain let out a yell as he went over the side towards the gray ship that lay low in the water. The whale surfaced under the captain, sending him closer to the brig.

It seemed to Juan as if the Devil himself had come to the scene. Suddenly hundreds of dolphins were leaping around them and driving the captain toward the brig, while pushing the dory away. The men's oars were knocked about and they pulled them aboard. The dolphins were pressing the captain against the brigantine. Water splashed over the men, increasing the noise and confusion of the scene.

As the dory was forced back toward the *Esperanza*, Juan shouted to the men not to fight against the dolphins. "Let them have their way or we will all perish!"

Juan saw the captain take hold of a ladder that appeared over the side of the brig, and Santos clawed his way up and out of the water. Juan stared as the captain went over the rail and fell onto the brig's deck.

Santos drew his blade, and Juan could hear him cursing and shouting, calling for anyone aboard to show himself, but no one appeared. The captain looked back to Juan and shouted orders to put in again and come over to the brig. Juan couldn't hear the words; he only saw the gestures the captain was making. Juan now stood on the deck of his own ship. With the captain off the ship, he was in command. He stood terrified, his knuckles turning white as they grasped the rails.

The captain began to move about the deck of the ghostly brig. He cautiously made his way from one end of the ship to the other, all the while shouting for someone to show himself. He went again to the rail facing the *Esperanza* and called loudly for the men to come over.

Juan saw the captain walking on the deck and then returning to the rail, yelling something that couldn't be heard. Juan considered putting the dory out again.

Santos turned in time to see a dark hooded shadow glide across the deck, through a hatch and disappear. He ran after the specter, waving the blade as he dashed toward the open hatch. As he neared it, the cover slammed shut, only to be flung open again by the captain. He dashed into the passageway, where the dark innards of the ship forced him to stop for a brief second. The hatch again slammed shut, causing the startled Santos to jump. He tried to open the hatch but it would not budge. He banged on the wood, hard and unyielding as pitch pine. Juan had seen Santos enter the hatch and decided to wait to see if the captain returned to deck before he went over the side for a rescue.

The captain's fear began to work against him. He didn't know what lay ahead down the darkened passageway; a single candle at the far end gave light, looking hundreds of feet away. His breathing became rapid and shallow. He felt as one might feel seeing the coffin lid close over them. The smell of the ship was horrible, like nothing he'd ever experienced. He had only one direction to go-- down the passageway. With the blade before him, he stalked ahead. The only sound was his breathing. Salty drops of sweat dripped from his face and beard.

As he waved his blade from side to side, it struck an unseen oil lamp, which burst to life. The tiny flame illuminated his close surroundings. He removed it from the peg and held it high in front as he moved. He turned but saw nothing behind him, and when he turned to move again, the candle that had seemed to glow at the end of the passageway had disappeared. Two feet in front of him was a bulkhead; the passageway was a dead end. He turned and banged against the left wall, to find it solid. He spun around to find the wall on his right had opened up into another passageway. He took a step, then retreated immediately.

The passageway he had just emerged from had become a wall. The only way now was forward. The captain screamed but his voice seemed to carry no further than a few feet, there was no echo or response. Juan, standing at the rail of his ship, could hear the loud wails coming from the specter ship.

Captain Santos walked through a maze of passageways, the rotting stink of the ship filling his nostrils. He tried to get his bearings but blank walls kept him from knowing where he was in the stagnant air. The sooty oil lamp began to feel heavy, and the air began to reek of a damp death, the kind found when a body is pulled from the water. The captain's thoughts spun wildly as he called for someone or anything to show itself. The weight of the lamp grew such that he couldn't hold it any longer and set the brass lamp on the deck. Once there, the lamp's flame slowly dwindled until it went out, leaving him in complete darkness.

Juan now heard another kind of scream and was terrified at what could have occurred on the ship lying just a few hundred feet away. He turned to his men and asked if any would accompany him over to rescue the captain. All of them backed away from Juan.

The captain stood motionless in the dark, waving the blade about and striking walls in all directions. He took a step and heard his feet slosh in the water that was beginning to fill the space. He struck out with the blade again until he found free air and stopped short, with his heart beating so heavily in his chest he thought it would burst. He heard a shuffling of feet just ahead and moved quickly in the direction, blade in front of him.

Bouncing off the wall and cursing the Devil himself, Santos saw a light in the distance. His bulk nearly filled the way and the rough boards tore at his clothing; his arms were bleeding from the ripping of the flesh. The light was coming from a source around a corner nearby. He warily looked around the corner and spotted a candle on a table.

There were two chairs at the table. One was empty and seated at the other was a figure that men would say was a ghost, as Santos could see through the thin gauze-like presence. Santos slowly moved to the front of the hooded apparition. He couldn't see a face or even into the darkness under the hood. His arm raised the blade and with the force that would have taken a mortal man's head off two times over, he swung. The blade flew through the smoky vision and never touched a thing.

Santos groaned as the vision moved its hand in a
gesture for him to sit at the chair provided. The trembling
captain sat slowly, all the while looking at the secret host,
never so much as blinking an eye.

The phantom figure began to speak in a whisper, saying
"It is time for you to come with me." Captain Santos
roared that he and his crew were sailing in safety, with
a good wind and no danger, he wasn't going anywhere.
He knew who the specter was. He'd heard tales of men
who had seen and escaped from this shepherd of death,
which could take men in their prime away from country
and home.

"No," he yelled a hundred times, until his own voice
was just a hoarse whisper to his ears. The host's nearly
inaudible laugh seemed to echo through Santos' trembling
body.

Juan heard the captain's screams and ordered two
men back into the dory. He went to the rail and began
climbing down the ladder, then hesitated as he heard a
clatter from the other ship.

In the ghostly cabin, the captain's eyes caught sight of
a door nearby and he slashed the candle in half, sending it
to the floor. He made for the door, flinging it open.

Juan had leaped into the dory and the two men with
him rowed half way across to the ship. They jerked at the
sight of a figure that might once have been a man, but
appeared to be something else--they were not sure what.
The wild haired personage, standing at the rail, frantically
waved his stubby arms. The white mane spread around
his face like a ghostly aurora. The maggot-infested beard
tumbled to his waist in a twisted mass. Juan and his men
cringed at the red eyes that flashed at them. The men
thought this was the apparition of Satan himself, but Juan

spotted the amulet that Captain Santos always wore about his neck. The round silver medallion had been taken from a sailor just before the captain had him thrown overboard, bound hand and foot, for killing a shipmate.

The men, not waiting for orders, turned the dory around and bent their backs against the oars to get them safely back to the *Esperanza*. Juan saw the figure slump against the rail; the beard dripped the horrid creature's red spittle, to sizzle as it dropped into the sea.

The captain saw his first mate and two crewmen row away, leaving him alone to deal with the spirit from Hell that was below deck. He pleaded for their return, waving his arms and crying out. He thought the foul smelling demon holding him captive was the force that made them flee. He bowed his head against the rail realizing the hopelessness of his situation. They were not going to return. Santos saw the *Esperanza,* with sails furled, in the last traces of the fog.

Juan looked back as he climbed aboard his own ship. Even though there was no apparent wind, he saw the ghost ship's sail filled and it moved off. It carried the foggy ether with it. The wailing sobs that rolled across the water out of the fog burned into the memories of the *Esperana*'s crew.

The fading cries of Captain Santos came from another world.

A Bullet for Paulo

His eyes were shut; shut against the glare of the rising sun, against the day, against everything. Paulo grasped the cup of coffee in both hands and sipped the thick black liquid. He rolled the coffee over his tongue, savoring the taste until it cooled, then swallowed. He placed the cup on the table, waiting for the saliva to clean his mouth. He continued this ritual until the coffee was gone.

Paulo lazed in the warmth by the outside table. In 1811, Fernandina was a bustling Spanish town, but the small cantina at the corner of Commandante and White Streets was quiet. The cantina was not open, not at this early hour. Raphael swept the floor, sprinkling sawdust around and leaving it to soak up dust and moisture from the previous night. Most of the time he swept spilled beer or whisky-laden sawdust, sometimes it contained blood, but not often. Paulo didn't care.

Maria heated dishwater on the wood stove in order to wash the glasses. Occasionally, if she had some, she would use soap. A few minutes later, she got the hen's eggs and fried them in bacon fat. When the eggs were cooked, Maria put bread in the pan, making brown crisp bread laden with the remaining lard.

Paulo always sat at the table outside the cantina, never inside. He wouldn't think of that. This was his table. The morning meal was free, given out of pity, but they would never say that and, of course, Paulo would never think that.

Ah, the coffee is good this morning, Maria. She knows how to make it. Taste it, Paulo, it is so good. Let it roll around in the mouth, si, like that. Smell the bacon, Paulo. Today maybe is the last time. Si, Paulo, maybe the last time.

Maria brought the tin plate and laid it in front of Paulo. His eyes were still closed. He said nothing. *Thank you, Maria, you are very kind. Tell the hen thank you.* Maria moved away, not even casting a glance at him.

Paulo's eyes were mere slits as they became accustomed to the bright sun. With head bent forward, he looked at the plate. *Ah, Maria, you are an angel. Today, Paulo, today might be the day. No one will notice for a while. Then what? They will dig a shallow grave and roll your body in for the worms. Right now, Paulo, drink the coffee and eat the good breakfast.* He picked up the nearly clean fork.

Paulo sat alone. No one dared to talk to him. Men walking to the wharves or shops would cross the street before they reached him so as to not pass near him. Most of the women stayed on the opposite side of the street. A few older señoras would walk by and not pay him notice. *They are the crazy ones. They still think I killed that Raul in a jealous rage. I hit him, God took his life. Ave' for Raul. The Jefe says I didn't kill him.*

The sun rose higher to hide behind the tree growing at the edge of the cantina's low tabby wall. The crisp ocean breeze rolled across the eastward sand dunes making the limbs dance. Paulo looked up and beheld brilliant golden dots of sunlight through the vibrating leaves. Maria refilled the coffee cup and left. *Gracias, Maria, you are truly an angel. They don't like you to feed me. They think I am a stray dog and you keep me around by feeding me. If you didn't feed me, they say I will go away. Ha! But today maybe I will go. I know how to go, it will be very easy. I have the pistola.*

The children of Fernandina ran on the dusty street to the mission school. Some just looked at him, others repeated names they had heard parents say. They laughed and ran faster. A woman sweeping the cobbled sidewalk yelled to the children while shaking the broom at them. One little girl, about ten years old, loitered by the low tabby wall beside him. The large dark eyes watched Paulo. She wasn't afraid of him. *Beautiful child. You could have been my grandchild. I am not crazy or a killer. They have made me into something I am not.*

Paulo watched her amble toward school. Every morning she would pass by, and every morning with the sunlight gleaming off the black hair, the doe-eyed girl would look at Paulo in silence. *She knows I didn't kill Raul. God took him. I just hit him. Beautiful innocent child.*

Paulo never looked far enough to see Fernandina's life emerging from the night's slumber. The energetic laughter of the children disappeared into the school. A baby's cry filtered in from a distant casa. A wagon passed, sometimes. His back was to the cantina and he could look down the street to the few buildings that housed a tiny garrison, guarding the sound that separated Spanish Florida from the English lands, now called the United States. That is, he could look at the garrison if he wanted, but he didn't. Paulo could hear her coming now but he didn't turn to see.

Each day, Esperanza, young, beautiful and lissom, would walk by and pass next to the wall. His wall. She never spoke to Paulo, he never spoke to her. Their eyes never met. As he heard the sandaled feet approaching next to his wall, he would look up to see the profile of Esperanza.

Who is this woman? She torments me. Does she really exist or am I crazy, like they say? She never turns to see the old man sitting here. I see the lovely full breasts and when she moves, she moves like my Rosa. I see you, Woman, hips swaying in the sun. You're torturing me, just like my Rosa.

He gazed at the woman walking away from him. He saw her silhouette through the sunlit cotton dress. *Ah, Woman, why do you come, to make me think of my woman who is now gone? I wanted her to stay. She left after God took Raul. She was as lovely as you, woman. Every morning you pass and stir the old man's passion. Passion? Ha! You stir the old man's memories, woman, nothing else. Today may be the last day. She was an evil woman. If she could not control the temper, how could I? But, ah, that was long ago, wasn't it? I must go now. Ah, the coffee was so good.*

Paulo stood, shuffled away from the tiny courtyard and east on White Street. Dust rose behind his slow moving steps. On the path to his shack, at the very edge of town, he brushed aside the overgrown weeds. With effort, he went up the two steps. *Maybe today, Paulo, eh, maybe today.*

He entered the hot, dusty one-room dwelling. There was no light save for the dirt-encrusted window, which grudgingly allowed a dim shaft of weak sunlight to enter.

He took the half-smoked cigar from the table, lit it and sat down. He puffed slowly, closed his eyes and waited. *Why are you waiting, Paulo? No one will miss you. They will dig the shallow grave and roll you in for the worms. Finish the cigarro, Paulo. There is time.*

Slowly, and with great satisfaction, he inhaled twice more, then rose. Paulo stared out of the window for a long time, toward the marsh and beyond it, to the blue-green ocean rimmed with glistening white sand. Palm fronds rustled and uncaring birds flitted among the live oak branches outside his window. He grunted, as if to say "so what," then turned to the bedside table, opened the drawer and removed the ancient pistol.

He cocked the hammer, raised the pistol with trembling hands and looked down the barrel. His thumb moved to the trigger. *Today, Paulo? Today?*

His thumb pulled the trigger.

Paulo, tomorrow I may buy the bullet.

Gambler

Cord Williams knocked the trail dust off his clothes
with his Stetson hat. The horse moved away from the
little cloud and pawed the ground in front of the stable
near the river.

"Okay, fellow, I'll quit." He spoke softly to the big
black horse. The stable boy took the reins and led the
stallion to the shed, which promised hay and water.
Williams gave instructions as to where he'd be and moved
off toward the center of the little town.

The gray eyes squinted against the brilliant sun. He
slowly surveyed the port town and its layout. The streets
of Fernandina ran from the docks on the riverfront to
the edge of the Atlantic Ocean just a few miles eastward.
It was June of 1888. He'd ridden for three days through
forested trails, sleepy farm villages, railroad towns and
cattle grazing land, and then taken a ferry to reach this
north Florida island.

It was like a hundred towns that Williams had been
in during the 1870s -- all wanted to survive and worked
hard to do that. Williams figured this one might make it,
showing him two banks as he got off the ferry. There
were the normal businesses for a town this size, several
hotels of varying repute, along with the women who
stared boldly from behind dirty windows.

Williams passed several old men napping as they leaned
back in chairs along the wooden sidewalk. He recognized
them--maybe not them, but hundreds like them in the
gold fields of California and Colorado. Burnt-out old
fellows that chased dreams from one place to another,
never finding El Dorado, and ending up becoming a part
of the earth they cussed and hacked at for the precious
ore. Williams was glad he had gotten out while he had
some money and strength left. He was glad to be back in
the East where the weather was more agreeable.

The Willows Hotel had clean windows and the desk
clerk said dinner was at six o'clock sharp and "don't be
late, the Missus gets fretty at those who come in at just
any hour." Williams nodded and went upstairs past the
door marked *Bath*, to which he would soon return to get
the rest of the dust off himself. He looked out the room's
window at the horse and buggy traffic below.

He was sweating from the heat and, with no rain in
sight, he wondered if this was the place to settle down and
maybe start a shipping business, like his father. There was
a knock at the door and he jumped, hand on his gun.

"Yes?"

"Water's hot," came the reply from the other side of
the door.

"Thanks, I'll be out." He let his six-foot frame relax,
then he settled in the lone chair in the room. He struggled
to get his boots off and looked at the exposed big toe
protruding from the sock. *Can't let that do*, he thought.
Got to get some socks in the morning.

With the bath over and some halfway clean clothes on
his back, he stood in front of the small mirror. Reflecting
from the flaking silver backing was the image of a man
who wondered how much longer he could be on the

move. He ran his fingers through his hair, noticing the gray tinges at the temples. A woman he thought of often had told him the gray made him a good-looking man at thirty-five years.

He made sure he was seated at six to keep the "Missus" from getting fretty. His tablemates filed in and were quiet, which caused Williams to wonder if the Missus allowed talking. Directly in front of him a middle-aged couple sat down. They were dressed in duds like they were from up North and they had a ten-year-old boy in tow. He nodded to the lady who quickly turned her head away. The husband missed it completely as he was tucking a napkin under his chin. To his left sat a man not much over five feet tall, who seemed to be in charge of a much larger, swarthy-looking fellow; Williams figured they were into sales or thievery. An odd assortment of characters joined them.

Then, as if making a grand entrance, a strikingly beautiful woman appeared at the door and paused before being joined by a slim man in a tan suit.

Williams noticed the man sported a neat mustache and stood a little shorter than the lady. When the man smiled and nodded to the other guests, lines formed at the corners of his eyes. The lady he was escorting had large brown eyes and raven hair, curling and framing about the loveliest face Williams had seen in a long time. When a chair was pulled back for her to sit, Williams and a few of the other men stood. A fellow across started to rise but his wife's quick hand pulled his arm and made him sit back, slightly off balance so as to make his chair scrape on the floor when he plopped back into it.

As she sat down, the dark-haired woman looked at Williams for a brief moment. She paused long enough for the eye contact to make him aware of the slightly upturned corners of her ruby-red lips. He'd seen the beautiful women of Spanish descent in the Southwest. The ones not married to wealthy cattle barons often worked in bordellos. He couldn't figure where this woman fit in the plans of the man escorting her.

The "Missus," a large-framed woman, brought in the food in huge earthen bowls. "There's plenty of it and I don't plan on feeding the hogs with it, so eat up and enjoy." She seemed to give this out, not so much as an invitation as an order. Williams looked up at her and when he caught her eye, he gave her a wink. She gave a "humph" and returned to the kitchen to gather more bowls. Quiet conversation mixed with the sounds of the silverware.

Williams listened to pick up information that might be useful. The threesome across were headed up to Savannah, the two fellows on the left were out to get some money owed to the big man, who was paying the little guy to get it for him. Not much of their conversation seemed to make sense.

The exotic-looking brunette and the man she was with were a bit more mysterious. They said they were traveling to see the South, and not much information came from them. Over the years Williams had occasion to observe couples such as he figured these two represented. A slick card dealer off a riverboat and a good-looking woman to be a distraction, as well as being able to send discreet signals of what the other card players were holding. Williams called a man like this a dandy, someone whose crooked smile couldn't be trusted.

The meal was nearly over when the large hostess came in following the boy who cleaned off the table, and she laid out rhubarb pie for everyone. When she put Williams' down she leaned close and lingered long enough for him to notice her sweaty odor. He did, however, have a larger piece of pie than anyone else. Shortly, they all got up and praised the Missus.

All but one of the ladies went toward the stairs while the men moved into the adjoining bar for a smoke and "some spirits to mingle with the bountiful supper," as the little man put it. The lovely senorita lingered at the hotel desk and watched Williams as he sat down near a door that led from the bar to the wooden sidewalk. He returned the look and ordered a whisky and water. A gust of hot Florida air blew through the door.

He briefly turned over options in his mind and dismissed them all, save one; he had a job to do. In this quiet time he watched the sunset turn the storefronts into flame red tones that filtered through the dust-covered windows. Thunderclouds marched across the far marsh. The townspeople wanted some of that rain. Lanterns were lit and placed around the barroom. Williams took careful note of where everyone was in the room.

A card game began in the far corner. Three lanterns hung over the table where five men talked and laughed. About seven-thirty, a man entered through the hotel door and leaned against the bar.

"How 'bout it, Gambler, you going to try it tonight?" came a question from the table.

The man called Gambler looked like a man used to traveling light and not staying too long in one place. "I don't know, I guess my luck's gone." The man's eyes slowly surveyed all the men in the room. He sipped the whiskey, then took a place behind one of the players. "You boys took real good care of me last night."

"Well, Biggman said he'd be in later, when he could sneak out of the house." The men laughed. Biggman was one of the bank owners, it seemed. The other bank owner was in the game.

Williams watched with interest as the game and talk unfolded. One or two of the low money players were out in about a half-an-hour. A few sailors and stevedores got in and out, losing quickly. Gambler sat saying nothing as he watched the game winnings move around the table, no one being a clear winner.

Along nine o'clock, a man called Biggman came in and found a hole at the table. He pulled out a wad of money and turned to Gambler. "Thanks for the stake." Gambler smiled and gave a mock salute.

"If I could come up with fifty dollars, I'd try to get it back." Gambler went along with the chiding he was taking from the other players. Hangers-on sat around as the game progressed, motioning to each other sometimes, a dangerous thing to do when the stakes get high, for no one wants any movement at the table area when a lot of money rests on the will and countenance of the players and watchers. Williams moved to the bar for a refill.

Gambler watched and called to him, "How 'bout a stake, cowboy, you got fifty? I'd have it back to you in half an hour."

Williams looked hard at Gambler. "You any good?"

"Yeah, he's real good," said Biggman, laughing.

Others chuckled. "Give him money and kiss it goodbye."

"I don't know, sometimes I play a long shot." Williams looked at Gambler.

"Half an hour, you'll get your money back." Gambler was almost begging.

The players looked at Williams. He paused, then went into his pocket, pulled out some scrip and gold coins, counted fifty and handed it to Gambler. "Half an hour, huh? Collateral?"

"Yep. Here's a gold watch my grandpappy had at Gettysburg."

"Better be." Williams put the watch in his pocket. "Half hour."

"Right." Gambler quickly moved to the table to fill the fifth hole. "I'm in, boys."

"And out." The players laughed.

Williams turned back to the bar and looked into the mirror. In the reflection he could see the dandy and the dark-haired beauty standing in the hotel doorway, watching the proceedings. Williams saw the red lips move slightly and the man answered. She looked in the mirror and noticed Williams watching them. He saw the setup. A real gambler comes into the game late and with his beautiful woman, drawing attention to herself and away from him as he skillfully plucks the chickens.

The dandy and his lady sat at a table near the game, waiting for a hole. Williams stood at the bar, amused at the play about to unfold. Around him he heard accents ranging from Spanish to Greek, Irish, Norwegian, and the drawl of America's South. Fishermen, sailors and various town characters came and went, always stopping dead in their tracks when they saw the dark-haired lady sitting in the warm glow of the lanterns. She did draw attention. Williams hadn't seen her slip out, but now she wore a ruby-red low-cut dress, revealing an ample cleavage. The clock over the bar rang ten o'clock. The dandy found a hole and was in the game.

Williams went to an empty chair behind Gambler

and watched. The nearly-in-tune piano was played by someone who hit nearly every note right. For some reason there wasn't much in bar traffic, mostly everyone was watching the game or the woman. The pile of money on the table kept getting higher and higher as the night progressed. It seemed that one of the bankers was having a run of good luck. The only stevedore still in was losing quickly and bowed out.

The winning banker spoke to Williams. "You want in, mister? Empty seat." He motioned to the recently vacated chair.

"I don't bet against my own money. Gambler here seems to be getting ready to give me a watch."

"Here's your fifty," Gambler said quietly. "That leaves me with about fifty. Poor winnin's."

"Deal. Let's see whatcha got." The winner was eager.

"Well," Cord Williams drawled, "I was willing to let Gambler lose my fifty; I may as well enjoy its company before I lose it to you card masters." He moved to the empty seat. Now there were the five, Gambler, the two bankers, Williams and the dandy. The woman sat behind the dandy, not moving. The Irish seaman who had recently lost got a whisky and moved in behind Williams, who looked over his shoulder and studied the man for a minute, then turned back to the table.

"Five card draw, nothin' wild. Ante five." The winning banker introduced himself to Williams. "John Murphy... Mister?"

"Williams...Cord Williams from the gold mines of Colorado."

"Well, Mister Williams, nice to make your acquaintance. This here is a bank owner, George

Biggman, and Gambler you already know, and I missed your name, sir," he said, turning to the dandy.

"Turville, Malcolm Turville--fresh from the wheat fields of Illinois."

"Well, Mister Turville, read 'em and weep. Now we know each other, let's play."

Each man drew his cards close and read his hand.

"Open." The clink of coins followed.

"Take two."

"One."

"Three."

"Two." The flap...flap of the cards was heard. Serious card playing began.

"Opener bets ten."

"Call."

"Call and raise ten."

"Call."

"Fold."

"Opener calls and raises five."

"Call."

Williams looked at the small two pair. Hesitantly he said, "Call."

To his left Murphy said, "Fold." It passed Turville to Gambler.

"Well, let's see. Five to me. Hmmm. See." Gambler pushed a coin to the center. "Mister Biggman, to you."

Banker Biggman studied his cards, then Williams and Gambler. Only those three were in now. "Call." He pushed a coin out on the table.

"Three jacks." Gambler laid out his hand.

Williams folded his cards and pushed them into the discard pile. Biggman looked at his three tens and cursed. "Damn, boy, how'd you do that? I'm a poor man and you're taking my money," he said with a poke in Gambler's ribs.

"Night's young, Mister Biggman, you might get it back."

"Hope so... deal."

So the game went. Back and forth. Williams was up several hundred as Turville began to show a little trail of sweat running down his sideburns to his chin, only to drop onto his expensive coat. He was only breaking even and Williams watched as Turville tried to look unconcerned that he couldn't get the cards to fall his way. Williams saw several slips in his dealing that someone with a lesser eye would miss. He'd seen all the tricks in the mining camps and used a few of his own once in a while. Tonight he was enjoying seeing Turville sweat.

Occasionally Williams turned around to look at the man behind him. The tall man with the weather-beaten face only looked back with no expression to read.

About eleven o'clock the sailor asked, "Mister Turville, have you ever been in Charleston?"

Turville glanced at him. "Not in many, many, years. My pa was killed there by a drunk Frenchman, so me and Ma went back to the family farm in Illinois. Been there ever since. Why? Do I look familiar?"

"A little." The sailor didn't say any more. Williams stole a look at the lady. She noticed his glance and gave him an alluring smile. Williams turned his eyes back to the game.

Williams dealt. "Ante five, boys."

The game went on. The bankers were losing slowly while Williams and Gambler were winning, but Gambler was getting most of it. Turville's sweat was beading on his forehead now and his collar was wet. He was losing about as quickly as the bankers. He had two hundred dollars in front of him, after having nearly a thousand one time.

Williams heard the sailor's chair fall from the two legs he'd been leaning back on to all four. Instinctively Williams' hand went right to his gun. He waited for a sound. Everyone at the table saw it.

"Bit edgy, Mister Williams?" Biggman said, "No need to be here. We're a quiet, law abidin' town."

"That's right," Murphy chimed in.

"Sorry. Sudden sounds get to me sometimes. Never did like the sound of dynamite goin' off."

"Understood. No harm done," Murphy said. "Deal."

The sailor went outside and in a few minutes came back with the sheriff. The sailor went to the bar, as the lawman touched Turville on the shoulder and leaned over to whisper in his ear. "Excuse me, gents." They both moved toward the bar.

The game paused, until Biggman said, "Deal, he'll catch the next hand."

Williams folded quickly with a little pair and watched Turville use his handkerchief to wipe his face clean of the sweat. The dark-eyed beauty never changed her graceful posture as she watched the game. Shortly Turville came over to the woman and whispered in her ear.

She rose and left the room. Turville collected his few hundred dollars and said, "It's been a good night, gentlemen. We have to rise early." With that he turned and dropped twenty on the bar. "Drinks on me, good bartender." He was out the door quickly and his footfalls could be heard going up the stairs.

The sailor sat in the empty chair. "I knowed I seen him and that woman. They took a group of sailors out of Boston for nearly all their pay up in Charleston by the waterfront last year. I know 'cause I was one of 'em."

Williams watched the reaction of the men at the table. "Damn," exclaimed Murphy. "Never know who's at your table."

"Nope, sure don't," Williams agreed.

The sailor got up and no one took the chair. Gambler moved it out of the way and now the four were squared to each other. The clock rang out midnight.

"Gambler, your luck has returned. I've been here all night and am barely even. That's no good. Loosen up, boy." Biggman enjoyed the Gambler's company. He nudged him on the shoulder. You could see Biggman envied the freedom enjoyed by Gambler. He wanted to share in it, even if only at the card table.

"I'll try, Mister Biggman."

The game went on. Murphy was losing even more now and dug deep in his pockets. He made foolish bets, hoping to recoup his losses. Biggman and Gambler were getting his money. Williams stayed about three hundred ahead.

"I'll be damned, I don't understand. I was doin' good early on," Murphy whined.

"Don't fret, John-- in the long run, it'll balance out. Whatcha doin' in town, Williams?" Biggman was feeling good about the pile of cash in front of him.

"Like I said, I left the gold fields with a little money and I'm looking for a place to settle, maybe give the shipping business a try."

"Ever done it?" the sailor standing nearby asked.

"Yep, after the war. My daddy's in the business in Virginia. I helped him when I was a lad."

"If you need a man, I'm him."

Williams met his eye, paused and said, "If I stay, you got it."

Williams dealt. "Ante twenty." Gold coins fell on the table. He looked to Murphy. "Open?"

"Twenty."

Gambler dropped his coin in followed by Biggman. Williams pushed his gold in. "Cards?"

The piano player came back from his free beer and played softer now.

"Two." Flip-flip.

"Three." Flip-flip-flip.

"Two." Flip-flip.

"Dealer take one." Flip.

"Opener bets twenty."

"Didn't make the flush or anything. Fold."

Biggman paused, studying his cards. "Call and raise a hundred."

Williams looked at the three queens and pondered Biggman's sudden bravado. "Mister Biggman, I want to take your money. Call." He smiled at the man.

"You're running my well dry, Biggman. Call." Murphy lit a cigar.

Biggman grinned and chuckled as he laid out a small full house, a pair of deuces and three threes. "Ain't it terrible to win with that little bit of crap?"

Williams pushed back and said, "Kicks my ladies in the ass. Bartender, whiskey and water and whatever these gents want." He flipped the bartender a ten-dollar gold piece and went out the back door. In a few minutes he came through the door, buttoning his pants. They all seemed to have agreed on a break. The bartender set down clean glasses along with a new bottle of whiskey and a jug of water.

Williams looked up as he heard footfalls on the stairs. The man who called himself Turville led the woman toward the door and carried their luggage out. They turned to go up Centre Street toward another hotel.

Biggman ignored the departing couple and rubbed his hands together after walking around the barroom. "Deal."

Murphy dealt. "My last hand, boys, unless I win the table."

They chuckled and tossed the double eagles in the pot.

"Open for fifty," Gambler said.

Murphy looked at him. "You're feeling awful lucky, ain't you?"

Gambler looked back and shrugged his shoulders.

Biggman tossed in his fifty. Williams pushed his in and Murphy studied his cards until Biggman said impatiently, "Either in or out, John. I got an early day tomorrow."

"In." Clink went the coins. "Cards?"

"Two."

"Two."

"One."

"Dealer takes three."

Gambler shuffled his cards for a second or two, then opened his hand. His face revealed nothing. "A hundred."

Biggman looked at his hand and at Gambler. "Boy, I believe you're bluffin'. Call."

Williams looked at the little straight flush he'd fallen into. "Well..." He knew he had the hand. "See the hundred and raise." He paused as he counted out the money. "One fifty."

Now it was Murphy's turn to sweat. He hated to lose, Williams could see that and knew Murphy was going to stay. He'd gotten bit and hung on with the tenacity that caused many a man to lose a lot of money. Williams watched.

"Damn." Murphy fingered the cards hoping to change the numbers on them. He looked at his small pile and at the cards, then at Williams. "And I believe you're bluffin'."

Williams had laid his cards down while waiting and now put his palms up and shrugged his shoulders.

"Call," Murphy said.

Gambler tossed in his money. Biggman looked again at his hand. "You two boys are crazy and I am here to take your money. Call."

Williams turned over the seven-high spade straight flush. The piano player stopped playing to see the results of the hand. Murphy took his handkerchief and wiped away the sweat. "It's been fun, and you boys, and you too, Mister Biggman, can kiss my ass good night."

"Night, John. I'll pass on the kiss." Biggman tossed his cards in. "I had another full house, too."

Gambler didn't say anything. He pulled in the cards and shuffled them. He looked at Williams. "Good hand."

Williams nodded. "Lucky draw, inside."

Gambler hung his head and shook it.

"You seem to be a bettin' man, Mister Williams." Biggman lit a small cigar.

"On occasion. I need to be pretty sure of the outcome or at least know if I can do fairly well."

"Well, let's say we start playing real poker? A man don't get the name Gambler by punchin' cows, does he?" He again nudged Gambler.

"No, sir, Mister Biggman, I guess he don't."

"Well, Williams, whatcha say?"

Williams looked at the pile of money he had in front of him. There must have been better than two thousand dollars there. That, coupled with the ten thousand he had in a bank in Atlanta, would go a long way in starting a shipping business. He paused, took a drink of the whiskey and water.

"What the hell, Mister Biggman, I want your money too." Williams stared Biggman in the eye, not smiling.

Biggman narrowed his eyes and then started to laugh. "Boy, you almost had me; let's play cards. Deal."

The game went on. The barroom had seven people in it, besides the bartender and piano player. They were napping on the hard chairs, only stirring occasionally when someone wanted a drink. The clock struck one o'clock. The sailor sat silently watching the game.

The piles of money moved only slightly during the hour to two o'clock. It was Biggman's deal. "Ante a hundred." Clinks followed. "Open?"

Williams looked. "Check."

"Open. Two hundred." Williams folded and the rest fed the table.

"Cards?"

"Two." Gambler put his draw on the end, not showing where they fit in the hand.

"Dealer takes, umm, two."

"Opener checks."

"Two hundred." Gambler shoved his money out.

Biggman's face took on a new look. Williams saw he was in a game where he liked to be now; he warmed up and loved every minute of the high stakes. It was a stimulation to him to risk the danger of the cards. Williams noticed the little veins on his temples stand out a little more. Williams looked at Gambler, who shifted in his chair.

"See your two and raise three." Biggman pushed the money out.

Gambler looked at the pot and then at his cards, finally to Biggman. "You took two cards and I took two cards. What does that tell me?" Gambler asked of no one.

Gambler smiled and leaned forward. "Just to keep us honest, Mister Biggman, see your three and raise three."

"Ha," Biggman tossed his head back. "I love that boy. Call."

Biggman looked at Gambler's kings-over-queens full house on the table.

"Damn, you're good." Biggman didn't show his cards. "Deal."

Williams dealt and the game moved on to higher and higher stakes. Soon there were four-, five- and even a six-hundred-dollar bet. Biggman began to lose. Gambler was winning and Williams was only up five hundred now. The clock struck three. Biggman began to lose more and more, causing him to make foolish bets on hands that had no chance of winning. To Williams that was one time that a man becomes pathetic, he bets foolishly and everybody knows it. Williams' pile of money began to grow larger.

Biggman was down to a few hundred dollars. Williams saw the resignation on his face; he'd been up nearly four thousand dollars and now was down to these few hundred. Biggman stood and stretched. "Gambler, Mister Williams, let's deal a few of showdown'."

"Mister Williams?" Biggman looked at him.

"Well, usually I like to have a say in how my hand is played. Maybe a hand or two to get you back in."

"Fine, deal, but I don't really like to do that," Gambler said.

Biggman's luck was remarkable. He won three times

in a row and was up to a thousand quickly.

"Enough of this, boys. Let's play cards." Biggman looked at Gambler and dealt.

"I'm gettin' a little sleepy, men. Soon?" Williams asked.

"Yeah, a few more." Biggman was revitalized, his eyes moved back and forth across the table.

Gambler dealt. "Ante. Three."

Biggman said, "Open. Two."

"Cards?"

"One."

"Two."

"Dealer takes three."

"Bet two."

"Fold."

Biggman said, "Come on, boy, don't be bashful."

"No sir," said Williams, "when they ain't there, they ain't there."

"True, true... how 'bout you, Gambler?"

"See you and raise five."

Biggman looked at him. "Call."

Gambler laid out two pair. Biggman smiled and laid three deuces on the table.

"Listen, boys, whatcha got there, about two thousand each?" Biggman dug in his pocket and pulled out a wad of money. He looked at his table stakes, then peeled off some scrip. "Here's two thousand. One hand." He pushed the money in.

Williams looked at Gambler. Gambler said, "I've got a good horse and Mexican silver saddle plus a thousand in my boots. Let's make it five thousand."

Williams drew in a deep breath.

"Hot damn, boys, sounds like fun," Biggman snorted.

"How 'bout it, Mister Williams?"

"I don't know, I guess I could. I hate to lose that much. I hoped to stake my business."

"Hell, settle here and I'll loan you the money for that. If you win, put your money in my bank."

Williams saw the vein pop out on Biggman's temple. "Okay." He knew Biggman was nervous and getting some sort of deviant pleasure out of it.

The bartender and piano player woke up and the remaining barflies sat in the chairs at the edge of the light. The room was silent. The sailor moved in closer.

"Your deal, Gambler." Biggman shoved the cards to him. A trickle of sweat rolled down his neck.

"Ante your stake." Gambler shuffled slowly and deliberately dealt slowly. Each card snapped as it came off the deck, then fell softly to the table. Williams let them fall, not picking any up until the last one fell. Biggman snatched each one up as it fell. Williams watched Biggman as he viewed his cards. Biggman's eyes jumped around the cards he held. It told Williams all he wanted to know. Williams and Gambler picked their cards up together.

The air was stagnant with the cigar smoke. One of the observers coughed. Williams looked at him. He ducked down, not wanting the stare. Lanterns around the barroom had gone out, but the three over the table were larger. Their soft yellow glow cast dim shadows to the floor of three intense men sitting at the table.

Gambler spoke softly, "Cards, gentlemen."

Biggman looked at his hand, his eyes still danced. Then he said, "Two." He tried to put his best face on but Williams knew he was out of it. Flip-flip.

"Mister Williams?" Gambler looked at him.

"One."

"Another inside?" said Gambler. Williams looked him in the eye and smiled.

"Dealer takes three."

Each man was now alone with his thoughts, figuring his odds against what the other men had drawn. Biggman, seeing Gambler take three and Williams take one, liked his chances better. He sat up a little straighter. Williams laid his cards face down and took out a little cigar, lit it and blew the smoke up at the lantern over his head. He looked at Biggman, who looked back with a questioning glint in his eye.

"Mister Biggman, do you run your bank this way?"

"What do you mean?"

"Gamble with other people's money so quickly."

"All this money is mine I've had tonight."

"I'm sure."

The pause broke some of the tension. Williams picked up his cards. Biggman looked at him with a frown.

Biggman spoke at length. "Well, I guess you want to see my hand." He laid down two pair, kings and nines.

Williams drew on the cigar and laid down three queens. "Maybe the ladies will be good to me this time."

No one spoke but both looked at Gambler. "It's been a long night and I thank Mister Williams for the fifty-dollar stake." He turned over his cards one at a time, showing five diamonds. Biggman let out a gasp and paled a little.

Williams' hand flew to his gun and drew it. The action caught everyone by surprise and woke up the drunks. The .44 was pointed at Gambler's face.

"Just a minute. It was fair and square," Gambler said quietly.

"I'm afraid so, Mister Williams." Biggman's eyes were wide open, the corners of his mouth twitched.

"Sailor, reach in Gambler's coat sleeve and remove those cards." The seaman moved and grabbed the right sleeve, shoving his hand up it. Slowly he removed three cards and threw them on the table. Williams cocked the Colt. None of the cards from the sleeve were diamonds.

"Mister Williams, has he been cheating all night?"

"No, not his kind, he's too cautious. He waits until the last hand when the stakes are high and he makes his move. But not too good tonight, Gambler. I ought to shoot you. What are the rules here, Mister Biggman?"

"We ain't never had to deal with this before," he said nervously.

Several men moved away from the table. Williams stood up and motioned for Gambler to do the same. The sailor spoke, "It's your call, mister--by rights you won the hand, and I'd plug him right where he stands."

"Is that right, Biggman, I win?"

"Why, yes, I suppose so."

Gambler's hands were up and he pleaded, "Let me go. I'll leave town, honest. Right now."

"Mister Biggman, when was the last time a man died in a barroom hereabouts?"

"About a year ago, Billy Crawford's wife shot him in the groin for fooling around with a whore. He died the next day."

Williams looked at Gambler whose voice was hoarse now. "I'll go right now, honest. I'll get mounted up and ride out."

Williams looked around the room. Other than the sailor's grim look, there was no indication that they wanted blood.

"Get out of here. If I'm to settle down here and I ever see you again, I will kill you. Understand?"

"Yes, sir." With that, Gambler was out of the bar in four strides. The door swung shut behind him. Everyone breathed again. Williams released the hammer on the huge Colt .44 and holstered it.

Biggman began to gasp. "I ain't never seen a man shot to death, and I am glad I didn't see it tonight. Your money is on the table, Mister Williams. I expect to see you soon in the bank." He shook Williams' hand and walked out, putting on his Stetson.

"I'd a shot him," the sailor spat out.

"Well, he may have deserved it, but some day he may show mercy on some poor sodbuster up in Georgia and not take all of his money." Williams stuffed half of the money in his pocket, the other half into a cloth pouch.

He walked out of the bar into the darkness. The bartender pocketed the double eagle Williams had tossed him and set up drinks around. Williams went to the edge of the porch and lit another cigar. The only light on Centre Street at this hour was the red glow of cigar embers. The spark of light traced a crimson arc from his hips where he hooked his thumb to his mouth, then glowed bright red as he inhaled.

He heard a rustle coming from behind him, in the small alleyway next to the bar. He tensed but felt the comforting weight of the Colt on his hip. With a slow movement of the forearm, he felt the handle fill his hand. The shuffling stopped about three feet away in the extreme darkness.

"How'd we do?" came a whisper.

"About four thousand each, I figure."

Williams held out the small cloth pouch filled with money. Gambler took the pouch and moved into the darkness. "See you in Savannah in about two weeks."

"Right." Williams made his way into the hotel for some much wanted sleep.

The Crying Children

This story could start by saying it was a dark and stormy night, but it wasn't. The stars shown brightly through the thin high cirrus clouds that promised a change in the weather. The moon was just rising over the Atlantic Ocean off Amelia Island, that little jewel of a barrier island in the northeast corner of Florida.

I was visiting a friend and decided to go for an evening walk along Atlantic Avenue. The warm summer breeze teased me with the ocean's sweet scent and all seemed calm. Auto traffic was light and the night pleasant as I made my way toward the ocean. I crossed over 18th Street and admired the stately oak trees in the failing light of day. Being alone I didn't want to stray too far from the path, so I could find my way back to my host's home.

The only sounds I heard were those of my footfalls. Lights began to appear in the windows of the homes along the way. I notice a particularly large oak standing alone in a front yard, and it had an odd look about it, if that can be said of a tree. The lower limbs were drooping, giving the tree a look of being sad and tired. I wondered if it were dying. I stopped and looked up to the higher branches, the ones near the top. As if stretched out in a passionate plea, those limbs stretched straight out with the tips slightly curled up to the sky.

Strangely, I began to sense the sound of crying--

almost impossible to hear at first. I guessed it came from the house, perhaps a young child inside. Then I saw a shadow move among the bushes near the house. I stood transfixed waiting for something, but I didn't know what to expect. Again, the crying child's voice drifted over me, but it wasn't emanating from the house. From just under the largest limb, that nearly touched the ground, came the sound of not one, but many children crying. Their tiny voices rushed to my ears, some calling out for "mama" and others lamenting in a language I didn't understand. Even in the warm evening air, I felt a chill on my back.

I don't know how long I stood there, but anyone passing in a car must have thought me insane. Ever so slowly the crying began to move away, yet in the same direction. The voices, calling out, were traveling into a tunnel, disappearing among the shadows.

I looked around to see if any other human being was nearby and if they heard the children crying, but I was alone on the sidewalk. With quick steps, I retraced my way back to my host and related the events.

He said there is a story, which is dismissed by nearly everyone, that when the French called this island Isle de Mai, there was a dispute between the European explorers and the native inhabitants. Tensions mounted as mistrust between the two groups grew until one evening, just after sundown, the French guards surprised the small tribal village near their own camp and killed all the inhabitants. Reports vary as to how many Indians there were. Some say only five or six but others say it was upwards of twenty-five.

My host continued by saying that there were other groups of Indians on the island, down toward the south end. Somehow, they had learned of the killing and were on guard all that night. The next day the French acted as if nothing occurred, and the captain visited the Indian campsite, down where the caution light blinks now at the end of the sentinels of oak trees.

In the early evening, the leader of the Indians gave the captain and his men food and drink. As the hours passed and the moon came up, the French were feeling happy from the mildly alcoholic drink the Indians had given them. What happened next is anyone's guess. The Indians had observed many of the white man's habits; one of them was the horrible fate of being executed by hanging.

The next morning, a group from the French encampment came into the deserted Indian camp to look for their captain. All they found, on a spot near where Harris-Teeter is now, were the remains of the captain's men and hanging from an oak tree was the captain himself.

The French took their own revenge. All Indians who had not fled were taken to a giant oak tree and there they were slain. The Indians returned to the island only when the Spanish came back, but throughout north Florida, the French were killed on sight.

To this day, said my host, there have been sightings of men dressed in tattered uniforms, walking among the palmettos looking for the French captain and his men. They pay no attention to people today and walk right past the living. Their eyes have a vacant stare but the heads swivel from side to side.

And, if you walk along Atlantic Avenue you can still see that gigantic oak tree, with the sad limbs reaching down to comfort the crying and dying children.

Stop and listen.

Wayne

The older man paid his five dollars to see the World War II flying museum pieces, here for one weekend at the Fernandina Beach Airport. The old B-17 sat dripping oil, as all round-motor airplanes do. Visitors lined up, eighteen to twenty people always in the line, to go through the B-17. Everyone who crawled through its cramped cockpit and other stations was enthralled.

A few wandered over to the P-51 Mustang fighter that sat alongside the bomber. As every B-17 crew knew, the P-51 saved many lives because of its long range and agility.

Walking around the big bomber, the man would glance at the P-51, not really wanting to look at it. It had been too long; memories were now forgotten. He had come out here because...he didn't know why. Wayne was now an insurance agent, had his own company in Fernandina Beach and was progressively giving it over to his son and grandson. He had places to go and things to do... play golf, not come here.

He heard a plane taking off from one of the airport's runways and looked to see a banner-towing plane pitch up to forty-five degrees, climbing to get the banner off the ground. At three hundred feet the pilot leveled off the blue Piper Cub to gain airspeed and made a shallow left turn.

He took a deep breath and avoided what in the end he knew couldn't be avoided. Slowly, mechanically, trying not to, Wayne was drawn over to the silent P-51. He said to himself, he could handle it.

He looked up at the cockpit, wanting to take a peek, but was stopped by the yellow nylon rope that cordoned off the cockpit area. His gray eyes retraced the Mustang's sleek lines, remembering every detail he knew so well. The twelve exhaust stacks were plugged with huge corks. When the Merlin engine came to life, those stacks would spit carbon and oil down the side of the fuselage. There would be a reawakening of life in those twelve cylinders.

Now it was asleep. A living thing, just sleeping now. He cautiously reached up and put his hand on the wing, felt the warmth of the metal. It seemed to move closer, such as a pet might move closer when you lay your hand on it, saying "hold me". His hand slid along the metal, caressing it, back and forth. He had flown many combat hours in one of these planes. He knew his plane better than he knew his wife. Most pilots did, good pilots anyway. You weren't a pilot and a plane; in the air, you became one.

The olive drab paint was flat, dirty and peeling where the sheer blast of four-hundred-miles-per-hour wind pried under its edges and ripped it off. Wayne slowly moved from the wing tip to the engine, never taking his hand off the warm plane. He felt its life, he could sense the sleeping pulse that was alive in her...he knew. He leaned over at the nose and saw the oil cooler down the center of the fuselage, a mark that gave the Mustang its distinctive graceful shape. His hand went up to the yellow spinner and down a black propeller blade and then back to the spinner. He again felt the warmth from the metal sitting in the sun. He moved over to the yellow engine cowling and aft to the other wing. His eyes never left the plane. He went past the three fifty-caliber gun ports to the wing tip, still caressing the plane. It seemed to reach out to him saying, "I understand."

"Wayne...break left...break left." He turned to see who spoke and no one was there. It was the voice of his wingman, some memory from the skies over Germany. His eyes focused on the canopy; the sun was a pinpoint of light playing off the Plexiglas. The brightness opened the safe where sacred memories are kept, hidden from those that don't understand.

"Wayne...break left...break left."

He instantly shoved the stick left and pulled back. The g-forces jammed him down hard in the seat. He grunted and tightened his stomach to fight off the beckoning call to blackout as the Mustang's wings went vertical and warped under the strain. He saw out of the corner of his eyes the German ME-109 pass overhead, and a second later, his wingman in hot pursuit. His wingman did his job, looking out for the lead and saving his butt. Randy Johns got the kill. The air battle was over. They rarely lasted more than twenty seconds. Later he bought Randy a beer; a squadron tradition, nothing more, nothing less. They each bought many beers.

The blue skies over Germany were alive at times. B-17s and B-24s would be on long penetrating raids and the P-51s would take over escort from the P-47s, whose range wasn't as long as the '51'. He'd seen men die and came close himself several times, but was lucky and came home alive. There were times he should have been shot down but his wingman was watching over him. No pilot could have wanted someone better. Memories hurt, but at the same time make us proud. The sacrifice is so dear.

"Wayne...break right...break right!!!" Once again in the headphones, Randy's voice crackled with static hiss in the background. This time when Wayne broke right, a line of holes marched their way across the wing to the cockpit and a round hit his shoulder. The brute force slammed him against the instrument panel and blood spewed from his face. The panel was a red polka-dot blur. In his daze he licked his lips and tasted the salty sickening results of his encounter with the metal panel. His right shoulder had no feeling and his hand would not move like he wanted it to. He took the stick with his left hand, pushed further right and pulled hard. He grunted and fought with all he had to stay conscious. In the dim gray light of beckoning unconsciousness, he turned his bobbing head to see the FW-190 over his left side, knowing Randy was close behind and, as if on cue, his companion's plane screamed past, guns blazing. Wayne closed his eyes, eased up on the stick pressure and opened his eyes again. Pain was now beginning to build up in the shoulder.

Suddenly he gasped as he saw a second FW-190, this one on Randy's tail. "Randy!! 190 on your tail. Break it off....break it off, bandit six o'clock."

No reply. The second FW-190 let loose with a barrage of machine gun fire and Randy's '51 belched smoke and started a climbing turn. As if in slow motion, the first '190 moved left, hard; Randy went up in a slow arcing climb to the right, trailing white smoke. It turned oily black after a plume of flame belched from the engine. The second '190 slowed to match the now wallowing '51 and fired more rounds.

"Randy, bail out...bail out!" No response came over the radio or from the plane.

The faltering P-51 seemed to stagger as it slowly came to a halt in its climb, hesitating for an instant as if on its knees begging for help. Finding none, the nose swung across the horizon and the plane began to spiral down. Occasionally it would try to stabilize; the wings would attempt to level themselves. Perhaps Randy was still alive, fighting to control the spiraling plane. Wayne watched as the Mustang went into a tighter spiral, then abruptly into a spin.

Wayne whispered "... get out... get out." Realizing ... struggles and wiped the tears from ... anger, pain, frustration, ... him, ... as the smoking spiral ... der ... No sound over the ... ce. ... his name ... he couldn't ... engine. ... his plane flew in and out of ... westward, ... other es... to Fort ... the ... wouldn't buy ...

The metal of the wing ... warm against his patch and Wayne ... this relic of the past, tears streaming down his cheek. He was suddenly aware of it and wiped them away to clear his vision. Watching him from the other side of the plane was a man. He also had a tear streaked face. As if on cue the two men started toward each other. Wayne for the first time let go of the plane and went to the back as the man came around the rudder.

They stopped and looked in each other's eyes, not

speaking. Slowly they lifted their arms and hugged each other. Tears dropped silently on the other's shoulder. They stood like this for only a moment, then stepped back, suddenly ashamed at this display of emotion. They looked down, shuffled their feet, and cleared their throats. The other man looked up at Wayne, their eyes met again.

"God bless them all," he whispered.

Wayne mouthed a "Yes, indeed," but nothing came out.

They walked side by side around the wing tip and away from the plane. The other man went one way and Wayne made his way to the exit gate and walked toward his car. He stopped to see the man approach his wife, who embraced him tenderly. The man's body shook slightly as the memories adjusted themselves in his mind.

Wayne turned, walked across the grass toward his car. A man in his mid-thirties, holding his young daughter's hand, walked by. She turned to watch Wayne go past and he barely heard her say above the wind, "Daddy, why is that man crying?"

"It's the wind, honey...the wind in his eyes."

Two-Finger Sam

This story is as true as you want to believe it. A few years ago, during an especially humid September in Fernandina Beach, my Florida hometown, I had an urge to get away from the heat and took a solitary trip out West. Late one afternoon, I traveled down a shallow valley in the outer reaches of Montana. To the west I saw the sun touching the snow-capped peaks of the Bitterroot Range nestled among the Rocky Mountains, just outside Dillon, Montana.

Four hours on the road began to wear on me and I looked for a place to get some food and a few minutes rest. Towns here are few and far between. I saw a light ahead, just off the road. I slowed, hoping it was a place to find something to eat and hot coffee to warm me against the coming snow. The dark snow clouds cautioned me not to be in a hurry. I also began to believe I was lost. I had made a wrong turn twenty-five miles back and needed directions to the main highway.

On a leaning post, a tired wooden sign hung nearly sideways; it read *Two Fingers*. I stopped in the dwindling daylight to see that the gas station/general store/diner was in the middle of town, as well as being on the outskirts of town. Two Fingers was a haven for any weary, lost traveler looking for a sanctuary who might find his way here. A dirt road bisected the hardtop road. Each direction of the dusty ruts undulated off into the focal-point distance. Light eased through the diner's window, beckoning me inside. I walked by three cars, the only ones on the gravel lot. Massive granite blocks beside the lot had thrust themselves up some eons ago in the building of the Rocky Mountains. These rocks and the building in the flat valley stuck up like a splinter might in the palm of your hand.

I sat at a clean red-and-white checker clothed table and perused the menu scrawled on the blackboard behind the bar. The faded chalk lines describing the cafe's offering probably hadn't been changed since the place opened. However, I did see some newer numbers in the top right corner that didn't make much sense, so I put it aside. My companions looked at me and I nodded to a couple with a baby. The dark skin and high cheek bones were characteristic of the Indians, or Native Americans, whichever you want.

The only other customer was an older woman with a shawl over her head. She faced the front window. I could only see her profile and that was beautiful in the low light. She ate quietly, her moves slow and deliberate.

The couple's baby began to fuss some. The mother tried to soothe the cries by offering a bottle, then by gently rocking the child in her arms, accompanied by an ancient lullaby. Whatever she did, the crying baby didn't quiet. From my parenting days I remembered colic in babies, but I remember the cries when a baby is just tired and wants to sleep. The husband's jaw muscles were clenching and he stared straight ahead.

A large man stood behind the bar, leaning on his elbows. He didn't say anything but just nodded toward me. I took that as a "What do you want?"

"Burger, fries and coffee, black," I said, and he moved off into the dark back room.

The wind began to pick up and whistle around the building. I'm probably wrong but the old place seemed to shudder a little. I hoped it wouldn't collapse on me and figured this place had lasted through some pretty bad storms. The level of the baby's cries and the wind just about equaled each other and, though one seemed almost to cancel the other, both were noisy.

"Snow," was the only thing the old woman said, looking up from her plate.

I looked outside and couldn't see the mountains and barely made out the outline of the cars in the lot just a few yards away. I didn't realize how quickly the weather could change. The large burger and mound of fries appeared in front of me, and the steam from the mug of coffee danced toward the ceiling.

The owner had quietly come and gone. He again leaned on the bar with his elbows and watched the snow fall for a minute, and then looked at the couple. His huge hands clasped together, toying with a small feather. His Indian features made me think of his ancestors who had this country until Manifest Destiny came along, pushing the white man westward. His lips moved ever so slightly but I heard nothing. The baby kept crying, even louder, it seemed.

I figured if I wolfed down the food I'd get out of here in short order.

Finished eating, I went to the bar and asked for a coffee to go. I paid the bill and asked directions to Butte.

The owner spoke softly, "I don't think you'll be going anywhere."

I said I'd try and headed for the door; snow or not, I had to get going. Upon opening the door, I found two feet of snow banked against the wooden frame. I closed the door and turned around to see the old woman was spooning the last of the soup. It was then I realized she was blind. The couple were apparently having words because of the baby's crying. I returned to the table, picked up the coffee mug and set it on the bar. It was quickly filled with the fragrant brew.

"How long do you think this will last?" I questioned the owner.

He looked at the counter, flicked a bug off and shrugged, "Maybe a day or so, it's hard to say. Sometimes it's just for a few hours since it's early in the season."

The old woman, silent until now, said, "He's coming."

Great! I thought, just what I needed. The owner looked up at the door with a jerk of the head. The old woman put down a piece of bread and waited. Slowly she cocked her head to the side as if she heard something not expected. Neither she nor the owner changed expressions until we heard the sound of crunching snow above the wind. Both the old woman and the owner focused their attention on the door. The wind had died down some; only the noise of the baby's cries and the soft crunch of footsteps surrounded us.

The door slowly opened; a man walked in, and I froze in place. He looked around the room from under a wide brimmed leather hat. Snow blew in behind him. He closed the door.

Before us was a giant from the past. I recalled stories

of mountain men and drawings of their garb. The buckskin shirt was darkened from the wet snow. The pants were also buckskin, as were the boots. Slung over one shoulder was a large leather pouch. In one hand he carried a Hawken rifle. A wide bladed knife was snug in a leather sheath on a strap tied around his waist. His blue eyes contrasted with the silver beard and hair that flowed from his head. He didn't speak a word but went over to the couple in the booth.

"Give me the baby." His words came from the bottom of a barrel.

The man and woman looked as shocked as the rest of us, not so much by what he said as by the whole scene that was unfolding. The man, barely twenty years old, just looked up at the newcomer. The woman held the crying baby close to her, arms encircling it.

"Give me the baby." His words were spoken again. He looked down at the woman, and as if in a trance she eased the crying baby away from her and handed it over to this rugged mountain man. He tenderly took the child, curling his huge arms around the soft blanket. He walked toward the old Indian woman, holding the child on the side away from me. His eyes were closed and he was whispering something to the baby. I could only hear soft whispers but couldn't make out what he was saying. It may have been a song of long-ago origin.

He stopped short of the old woman, turned around and started back toward the couple. He seemed not to be conscious of anyone as he soothed the child. When he was abreast of me I saw the hand that was against the baby's back had only two fingers and a thumb. The baby stopped crying and fell asleep. The huge man gave the infant back to the mother.

He looked down to the woman and said, "The baby will be all right now. It will sleep." With this said and without looking at anyone he walked to the door, opened it and walked out into the darkness.

"Damned if anyone's going to do that." The angry young man jumped from the booth and ran out the door. We could see him stop just outside and look around. "Where is he?" He shouted, "Hey, old man, where are you?" He came back and closed the door. The snow had stopped falling.

I looked up at the owner, who moved over to the menu blackboard and rubbed out the numbers on the upper right corner. He wrote a new one and looked at the old woman, who nodded to him; somehow she knew what he did.

I finally got my wits about me. "What the hell just happened?"

No one seemed to hear me. The couple got up and the young man paid the bill. The baby was enjoying a good sleep. The old woman drank from her coffee mug and turned her head to follow the sounds of the couple's footsteps as they went to their car. I looked at the owner and his blank expression indicated I wasn't going to get a response very soon. I stood and walked to the bar. I could hear the couple's car drive off into the night.

Again I tried to get an answer. "Who was that man and what's going on?"

The owner reached under the bar and brought up two small glasses and a bottle of bourbon. He poured some in each glass, still not saying anything. He paused, then began.

"That's Two-Finger Sam. He was married to a beautiful Crow Indian woman. They were on their way back to camp from tradin' furs when they were spotted by a band of rogue Flathead Indians. Two-Finger, his woman and the baby were chased for three days until they found a spot in those rocks outside the door. The Flatheads looked all around the rocks. But Two-Finger had hid them deep and covered them with what little brush there was about. They were almost safe when the baby started to cry and his wife couldn't stop the baby's wails." Here the owner took a drink of the bourbon.

"Well, the Flatheads heard it and dug them out of the rocks. They tied up Two-Finger Sam, killed the baby outright, raped the woman for several hours, then killed her, all in front of Sam. They recognized Sam and let him live. His reputation was that of a brave man. He had lived with the Flatheads for a season, but they'd realized he was dangerous so they had cut off his trigger finger and pinky."

I must have stammered because the owner pushed the glass toward me. I took a swallow and asked, "Did the police catch them?"

"Police?" he grunted. "This happened in 1837."

I had a hard time taking this in. "1837?" I looked up at the blackboard. The number 47 stood out in new white chalk.

He saw what I was looking at. "Yes, and that's the number of times he's come here. It's always to quiet a crying baby."

The Next Bend in the Road

Harvey Matson left his district office that fronted Centre Street in Fernandina. He looked up and down the winding, narrow street and thought this might be the last time he saw it. Tourists and locals alike meandered in the warm, golden sunlight to the shops and stores that were the pulse of Amelia Island's historic district.

He smiled at the cleverness of his nefarious deed aimed at his international employer. Where he worked doesn't matter, but his CEO and several vice-presidents would get a call from the IRS in the morning. Harvey had cooked the books in his favor at the expense of the twits above him. No longer would they overlook him for advancement. For years they promoted sons and sons-in-laws who didn't know squat about the business.

Well, he'd show them. That little fling he was having with his secretary would come to an end. When he disappeared, his wife wouldn't notice much difference in her daily life. Yes sir, he was going to be on Easy Street now.

Harvey went to a bank and, as prearranged and plotted, withdrew a large sum from an account he'd been filtering money into for years. Keeping a straight face, he explained it was to be given to a children's hospital. Cash was needed to show how generous was his company-- "for the TV people," he said.

Harvey sat in his car outside the bank and gave a chuckle at having pulled off a great feat. He watched everyday people filing in and out of the bank and thought what fools they were and how clever he was. The company auditor was staying at a B-and-B on the beach, at company expense, naturally, and would be coming into the office the next morning only to discover Harvey gone, along with a "few dollars of retribution money," as Harvey put it.

There was no hurry for him now; in fact, he walked over to Fantastic Fudge and bought his favorite ice cream cone and stood just outside the door watching people as they sauntered about.

Clever old Harvey, finished with his ice cream, drove down to the end of Centre Street, where people stood watching a shrimp boat ply the Amelia River. He swung around in the parking lot next to Brett's and headed to 8th Street and then south toward the causeway. Once he crossed the Shave Bridge he was really happy. He was on his way to Jacksonville's airport.

Harvey turned off I-95 at Pecan Park Road to take the back way to the airport. His car sped down the long road toward the distant airport, and he thought of the new life he would lead in some Caribbean island, unknown to anyone. Maybe a name change, he thought. He pondered options, thinking about what sounded like a good name for himself, now that he was a man of means. Harvey's thoughts floated as he followed the slight left curve in the road. He hardly noticed the youngster, about six years old, standing by the road watching his car zoom past. Harvey passed familiar landmarks, paying little attention to the road. Two miles later he followed the next gentle curve to the left in the road. He opened the briefcase on the seat next to him. Stacks of bills – five hundred thousand dollars -- smiled back.

Oh yes, he thought, what a wonderful time he would have. Maybe travel to several islands and have a girl waiting at each one. Harvey made another gentle curve to the left and continued on. There was a boy about twelve years old standing beside the road watching him go by. The boy stood in front of a nice house, set back a little off the road. Harvey hadn't noticed much, but it looked neat and recently painted. Harvey was in love with the world because of his cleverness.

He passed more familiar surroundings. Two miles farther, he made a gentle turn to the left as he glanced over at the money sitting next to him. The money looked different but he didn't know how. He kept an eye on his speed; he didn't want to be stopped with this money lying in the open. He saw a young man in his twenties standing next to the road watching him go by. Somehow the young fellow looked familiar. The house was in need of a paint job.

The road was smooth and quiet, with no cars. He again made a gentle left curve and looked at the money. He jumped a little, there seemed to be several stacks of bills missing. He looked up to stay on the road and saw an older man standing on the road watching him go by. The house behind the man was rundown-looking and the yard needed cutting. Little beads of sweat popped out on Harvey's forehead. Something was wrong, terribly wrong.

The car sped up. He looked at the odometer. The numbers read 10,988.7, so he was traveling; but he was going over the same route. He looked up ahead and saw the next curve in the road...to the left. He made it and looked at the briefcase and drew in a sharp breath. The money was half gone. He frantically looked at the rolled up windows. There was no wind in the car.

He didn't want to look at the side of the road, but he did. Standing just off the road was an old man watching him speed by. The house was dilapidated and nearly hidden by the tall weeds in front by the road.

Harvey's breathing grew rapid. His eyes widened as tiny beads of sweat popped out on his forehead. He searched the rearview mirror for headlights; he hadn't seen any cars since he turned on Pecan Park Road. He watched the briefcase at the next curve. Several stacks of money melted into thin air. Was that sound he made a whimper? Trickles of sweat ran down his blotchy face. It couldn't be happening. Things like this don't happen.

He was jerked back to reality, as he knew it, by his car running off the road. He fought the wheel and gained control. He was on the long straightaway now. He looked for someone standing beside the road but no one was there. He saw the house. It had fallen down and only the chimney was standing. Realization came to him. He slammed on the brakes but to no avail. The motor kept its purring sound. He tried to steer off the road, but of no use. Harvey pressed on the brake pedal as hard as he could, grunting with the effort. It didn't move. The car made the next curve in the road all by itself. And the odometer read 10,988.7, same as before.

The briefcase was empty and the car hummed along in the darkening night, always going left at the next bend in the road.

There was an article in the paper about money being found along the highway. The police interviewed a six-year-old boy who told them the preposterous story that he saw it fall from the sky as he was standing in front of his new house.

The Decision

I came to possess scraps of a journal upon a great-uncle's death. He knew of my interest in history and in his kindness he made me the recipient of the papers in his will. I sat on my front porch as I read these handwritten words.

I could not sleep; the weight upon my soul would not allow me rest. I heard a stir outside the tent and went to investigate. By the light of the small fire I noticed a soldier at post by my mount. He gently stroked the horse's muzzle and murmured in soft tones. He turned when he heard my approach. I had stepped on a twig.

He spoke, "Good morning, sir."

"Morning, son."

"I've been detailed to watch your mount."

"I don't recognize you. What outfit are you with?" I asked the boy.

"Company D, 3rd Regiment, Virginia Volunteers, sir."

"You've had it rough," I remembered.

"Yes, sir, but now it's over, isn't it?"

"Yes." I answered. I studied this boy. Most young men were afraid of me. Afraid may be the wrong word. I've seen them die for me, without questioning my motives.

His words came easy to him.

He turned to me and asked, "Are you sure this is the right decision, sir?"

I was taken for a moment by this forward question, but perhaps it had to be asked. Looking away, I replied, "I've lain awake all night asking the same question. Am I making the right decision? Is this choice the best?"

"I would think history will answer that, sir."

"I don't have a concern about history, son. My concern is now to save boys and let them grow into men." My insides hurt again. The recurring ailment was upon me once more. I don't know why I was talking to this young man, but I felt drawn to speak. He was indeed a man after living through the terrible fighting to which he had been exposed. I saw several camp fires begin to appear at the first gray streaks of dawn. Men softly cursed the day, the hour and each other. I hoped, no, prayed to God in his might and grace, to spare us in these next few hours.

I sadly looked across the field of tents and pondered how beautiful this meadow must have been when mist rose from it on autumn mornings. Smoke from last evening's fires draped itself over the hollow. Its shape remained motionless. I've always been spellbound by the mystery that at a certain time of each dawn, the world seemingly stops. I wonder if it's anticipation or a period of transition. The night birds and animals have returned to safe havens and morning creatures are not yet stirring. It is a time of truce. I wondered if, for me, it now was that time of truce between my conscience and soul. I closed my eyes, drew a deep breath and knew I made the right decision.

I looked back at the young soldier. "Yes, son, I made

the right decision."

"Yes, sir, I know you have." His voice was quiet, gentle. I hesitated to ask his age. His prodding questions gave him a certain maturity, one beyond the image his boyish face caused one to believe. For a moment I wished I were his age again, then dismissed this folly.

More campfires appeared as the smell of wood smoke filled my nostrils. I've grown so used to it now, almost to a point of dislike, but now in the cool of this morning, I knew it would be the last time under these conditions.

The gray sky gave way to the glow of pale yellows and pinks as the day bore upon us. I closed my eyes and prayed again to the Almighty for wisdom and strength. In the far distance I heard a dog bark, signaling dawn's quiet truce was over. Birds now called to each other from perches. Tin cups banged and still sleepy men stumbled about.

My aide approached and said, "The coffee will be ready in a moment, sir."

I nodded and motioned over my shoulder for the aide to see if the boy wanted a cup.

"Boy? Sir, there's no one there."

I turned and my mount stood alone. I inquired as to whom the guard was that had been posted for the horse.

"No one, sir, we saw no need in it."

Later in the morning, as my staff and I rode to the two-story farmhouse, men under my command stood and in an eerie silence saluted as I passed. Grown men who withstood cannon shot and musket ball for four horrible years let tears freely run down their cheeks. I thought I heard muffled sobs.

We slowly passed through our troops to the ranks of the soldiers of the other side. I was moved as they, too, stood and silently saluted. I must admit I felt a coolness run down my cheek, and through blurred vision, I returned the salute.

A young soldier took my reins as I dismounted. He looked familiar but I couldn't recall him, there have been so many. I was introduced to Mr. Wade, the owner of the farmhouse. He led my staff and myself inside his home. I had arrived before my counterpart and took time to look about the room.

It was a modest dwelling and functional for a successful farmer. A small round table was before the hearth with two chairs. Above the roughhewn mantle hung a charcoal drawing of a boy in uniform.

"Your son?" I asked Mr. Wade.

"Yes, sir, he died early on."

"I'm sorry." I didn't know what to say.

"Thank you, sir." He quickly turned and walked to the porch. It still must have been difficult to understand why these things happen.

I looked back to the portrait. The soft eyes of the sixteen-year-old boy looked out of the charcoal. They were the eyes of the boy who stood with my horse at dawn and that of the lad who took the reins moments earlier. I had looked into the eyes of so many young men, alive and dying, they merged into one face. I heard a cheer in the distance then it quickly subsided. I knew my counterpart had arrived.

Shortly all business at hand was settled and with a heavy heart I mounted my horse. The boy holding the reins hadn't moved in the previous half hour. I was yet to fully see his face but when he handed the reins to me, I saw he was the boy at my tent and in the portrait.

I was mesmerized. Mr. Wade stood alone on the

small porch to see us off. The boy left us to climb the porch steps and stand beside Mr. Wade.

I returned Mr. Wade's nod and I heard the boy say, "You made the right decision, sir."

I gently prodded Traveler's side. He turned and walked slowly toward my headquarters.

Turning back in the saddle I saw Mr. Wade standing alone on the porch.

The Wolf

Bill and I walked from the float plane toward the cabin, wondering why Jack wasn't at the dock to meet us. We flew here each spring to bring in the first supplies of the short summer hunting season. Jack wintered over here, as was his way, and opened this beautiful spot in the Canadian wilderness for a primitive hunting lodge a few months during the year.

We saw snow banked against the cabin; the ground hadn't been disturbed in a long while. We paused and looked at each other when we saw the windows had been boarded up, from the inside. Quickly we went to the door and broke the ice that had frozen the hinges. We entered the cabin and stopped short.

The body of our friend lay on the bed. He had been dead for a while, yet the cold had kept him nearly perfect. After the initial shock, we looked about the room for clues to the reason for this grisly discovery. The normally well-furnished cabin was bare except for the bed, a table and the wooden chair. Bill went over and covered the body with a sheet. The dark interior added an even more morbid feeling to the already unsettling scene. I went outside, took a deep breath and went back in to again survey the interior. Nothing made sense. We three had been friends for a long time, and this was the last way we expected to find Jack. We went back pretty far.

On a hot morning in Viet Nam, we'd sat together in a foxhole made by a five-hundred-pound bomb dropped from a B-52. Jack and I had just arrived in Viet Nam and were scared. This patrol was our third, and the first where we came under fire. Several of our patrol took hits and we called for help on the radio. Other patrols were in the area and making their way toward us. This was the first time I saw Jack's ability to perceive movement or something being out there when I couldn't see. He raised his rifle with a slow fluid motion and as soon as it was in position, fired. From the top of a tree about a hundred yards away, I saw a body fall. I asked Jack how in the hell he could see that man from where he was. He guessed he was lucky.

We were quickly reinforced and the VC patrol that had us pinned down disappeared in the jungle. I bragged to the company sergeant about Jack's shot and he was sent to sniper training, then returned to our unit as a sniper. He worked mostly alone and usually at night. He talked little about what he did, although he and I were close then and in the years since.

Back in the cabin, I noticed an open notebook lying on the table. I sat in disbelief and stared at the notebook, which a veil of dust covered. Barely readable words spoke of triumph and ended with Jack's signature. Something about this whole thing wasn't right. Jack knew how to live off the land, even the harsh winter land of Canada. He always was well stocked in case game was scarce. I flipped the pages back to the first page. The first two or three entries mentioned trapping some rabbits.

His entry of December 6 was different.

For the past two nights I heard the wolves. Last night they must have taken the prey; their attack could be heard over the lake, echoing and reechoing from the mountain on the far shore. I went to the dock and listened. The howling, for some reason, was unsettling. Their exact location couldn't be determined because of the echoing. I try to keep a fire going so the smell of the smoke will keep them away.

He said on the 10th he saw tracks and some game that was partially eaten. He knew the wolves were about the place.

On the 13th he had a slight run-in with some:

Hooray! I shot a small elk this morning. I don't understand why it was alone. It must have been a yearling because of its size, and it was pretty far from the normal trails. The fact it was young means it will be tender. Something strange happened while I was sledding it back. I heard the wolves yapping in the distance but I never saw them. They followed me the mile or so back to the cabin. I've scraped and hung the skin to dry. I guess I have 150 pounds of meat. That'll be enough for the rest of winter, with a bit of rabbit now and then. The early afternoon sunset brought a bright red sky. I hear the wolves howl in the distance and growls coming from where I dressed the elk. They must be fighting over the food.

Long ago, Jack told me about the sounds he heard at night while waiting to make a kill in Nam. He must have had nerves of iron. He had to sit still for hours. He said the worst sound was when he didn't make a clean kill. The screaming of the dying man almost drove him crazy at times. I asked him why he went back. He didn't know.

The next two entries in the notebook told how the

wolves kept howling. On the 23rd he heard sounds on the porch and some thumping against the door. At least he thought he heard them, but there was a terrible blizzard and high winds blowing in from the northwest. On Christmas day he had a great meal. He spent all day preparing his feast.

On December 29th and the next two days had startling entries:

Each morning for the past three days, I open the door, the wolf was there. On his haunches looking at the door, like he's waiting for something. Each time I ease back into the cabin and get the 30-06. Each time as I squeeze the trigger he moves just in time. Today I called the bluff. I got the 30-06 and put a porch chair in front of the door and sat down. We stared at each other for an hour. I saw the fir trees around him moving but didn't see any other wolves. What's their game?

The game went on today too. I sat there with the 30-06 for an hour, pointing it several times in his direction. He never moved. Tomorrow I may pop him. I saw movement among the trees, shadows of his followers.

Today after I ate, the devil returned. I sat for only a few minutes today watching him before I raised the rifle. When I made the move, slowly raising the 30-06, I saw others come out from among the low hanging branches of the firs. They all gathered around the leader and sat as he did, watching me.

I raised the rifle, sighted it, and he didn't move. He was calling my bluff. He died proud, but he died. Stupidity. He could have run but his pride overtook logic. The shot hit him between the eyes. The others disappeared in an instant. The leader flipped over backwards into a tree and lay in silence, not moving. It was a clean kill.

I sat for an hour or more, waiting for the pack to return, but none did. Taking the dead wolf by the neck, I dragged him out onto the lake, far from shore. He was heavy, surprisingly so since food was a little scarce and the pack seemed to be big. I laid an elk bone beside him.

Jack was well acquainted with the perils of the North Country and had been here about ten years running the primitive hunting lodge. He only allowed two or three hunters in here at a time. He said too many people made him uneasy. But the twenty or so people he had each year paid for the supplies for the winter. He was expensive but he was good, and his eye with the rifle saved more than one foolish hunter. I read further. On New Year's Day he wrote:

Last night's stillness was only temporary. Around midnight, I heard a wolf begin to howl. The horrible sound came from across the lake. It reminded me at first of a baby's cry, then wavered into a long howl. It kept on as though the Devil himself was crying. This went on for nearly an hour, and then they all started. The pack was holding its funeral service. It began to get on my nerves so I took the 30-06 outside and fired a round. Instantly it was quiet. The rifle's report echoed for long seconds up and down the valley.

It was only a short-lived silence after that. At first, there was only the lone cry again, then the others joined in. I came inside the cabin. The howling may have lasted, I don't know. I went to sleep. The shock came this morning.

When I went outside around noon, the elk bone was at the door. There were a few tracks in the new snow. One or more of them had come in the night. You don't realize the sudden fear you get when something like this occurs. I immediately got the 30-06 and took a quick look around the cabin.

I walked to several of the nearby traps and saw no tracks. I stopped and listened carefully for many minutes. I would hear shuffling among the trees, stop and listen, but nothing. Each time I stopped, it would stop. I think my ears were playing tricks again. They aren't that smart. I went to the lake and the dead wolf was gone. Apparently the pack dragged him off during the night.

He continued on January 2.

The wolves howled all night, again. It seemed to be closer this time. As dawn approached and I could see in the dim light through the frosted window, shadows moved on the snow. Soon the shadows took shape and one by one they emerged to sit along the edges of the trees, all looking at the cabin. I took the 30-06 down, made sure it was loaded. I flung open the door.

I raised the rifle and without really aiming I fired round after round. I quickly stepped onto the porch and wherever I saw movement I fired. When I stopped, the rifle fire resounded around the forest and across the lake. I stood on the porch for at least five minutes and nothing could be heard. I ventured out to where they had sat, to see if I hit any of them. I guess I was firing with so much anger that I missed them all, for there was no trace of blood.

All day today I sat on the porch, waiting for them to return. But if they run true to habit, the devils will return in the night. They must really be trying to get back at me for killing the leader.

I don't know when or why Jack began to think the wolves were reasoning animals. Maybe because they were the only intelligence he had any contact with during those long days. On the 6th he wrote the wolves had apparently left. He tended traps some distance from the cabin with no sight or sound of the creatures.

It was difficult to believe what came next. Yet he was never prone to making up stories. On the 7th he entered this:

Today I am lucky to be alive. They returned this morning. I am sore and exhausted. I was down on the lake, without the 30-06. I figured the wolves had left the area, so I didn't need to carry it. I scanned the lake with my binoculars and saw a small herd of elk down at the far pass, heading south. I started to return to the cabin and sitting in the middle of the path was a wolf, between me and the cabin. I froze for a second thinking over my options. I decided to circumvent the situation, and get to the cabin from behind. I looked through the binoculars all along the shore line. The wolf had no companions.

I started to the left and walked for several hundred yards and around the little crook in the lake, out of sight of the dock. I stopped, scanned the shore line and saw nothing. Keeping a wary eye on the shore, I moved on, and about half way, I saw movement in the shadows. The wolf appeared in the shadow of a tree. It seemed to be the same one. All I had with me was a knife and the binoculars. Of course the Bowie would take out one wolf at a time, but I didn't look forward to hand-to-paw combat.

I paused and then retraced the route plus about four hundred yards past the dock. When I passed the dock, the lone wolf had beaten me to it and was sitting there, watching me as if waiting for me to challenge him face on. I knew I'd win one on one, but there was a chance that its friends were still around and it would be a little tougher against two or three. I only heard the snow crunching

under my snowshoes. My steps made an arcing path
to the shoreline about two hundred yards ahead. High
bluffs, created by the rock outcropping, would offer
some security from attack on shore.

I put the glass toward the shore as I approached. Saw
nothing. I was close to the ledge of rocks where I spent
many sunny days catching fish. Now the ledge protected
me from a danger, perhaps lurking a few yards away. No
wolf in sight.

I hugged the rocks and moved away from camp to
where the ledge fell away to meet the shore line. It was
only a hundred feet away. I searched the shore to the
camp site and into the woods. Still nothing. Good, I
thought, I'll be in the camp in five minutes, get the 30-06,
and hunt the wolf.

On shore, I moved along the path toward the cabin.
It was nearly a straight shot to the door. I hoped the wolf
was long gone.

At the last little curve in the trail I looked down to
the dock. There sat the wolf, watching the lake. I had
fooled him. I was careful to not drag the snowshoes.
"Stupid wolf," I whispered. "When I make the cabin,
you're dead." I had less than a hundred yards to go. I was
closer to the cabin than he was but he was faster on the
ground.

Behind me I heard a low guttural snarl. I turned to
see another wolf about three hundred yards away. The
wolf at the shore turned and saw me. We broke into a
run at the same time. I struggled as hard as I could in the
snowshoes and drew out my knife. At last the ground
got harder and easier to run on. The wolf's huge paws
spread out on the snow and prevented him from sinking
in too deeply. On he came. Fortunately for me, at the

little crook in the path, the wolf decided to take a short cut between two trees. The snow had not been trampled down there and the wolf sank in the snow. I heard the wolf behind me calling to the others that must have been scouting the nearby woods. I was not a hundred feet from the cabin. Then the first one got free of the snow.

I could see fierce determination in his eyes. He snarled and I knew he wanted to make this a quick kill to the throat. He wasn't going to stop and wait for the others. I made it to the foot of the steps and was waiting for the weight of the wolf. I kicked off the snowshoes and stood, knife ready. He launched himself at me.

In an instant he was in the air. The jaws were wide open and a growl issued from his throat. Once he was in the air, I dropped down and thrust the knife upward; it was my only hope. I knew if I misjudged, I would have a fight for my life. The blade sank home deep within the stomach of the wolf. He stopped the snarling and fell to the ground. I couldn't relish any victory now because the other wolf was just a few feet away. I looked from the dying animal to see the second one airborne, attacking for my throat. I didn't have time to react as I did the first time. I shielded my head with my arm and fell to a crouch.

The second wolf sailed over me and landed on the porch, spun instantly, knocked over a chair and lunged lower this time. He caught me waist high and I slashed at the beast with the bloody knife. I couldn't seem to get a clean shot at him. He was growling and snarling wildly, venting his fury. His fangs had a vice grip on the parka and his paws were shredding the outer coat. He twisted and turned, violently shaking his head from side to side. I was barely able to keep my balance. I felt pain as a paw struck. *My blood warmed my face. I felt the wolf's hot breath in this frozen air. In all this confusion and madness I heard the yelp of the others on the run, hoping to get in on the kill.*

I struggled with my attacker, but I don't think my knife touched him. His thick winter coat not only protected him from the numbing cold, but prevented my blade from doing any damage. We fought for what seemed like a long time but could only have been long minutes. Several times we fell to the ground, rolling, tumbling, and flailing at each other, me with my knife and him with his sharp paws. I was nearly drained with exhaustion. My only hope was that he, too, was spent of energy. I felt my knees giving out. Wolves have tenacity that is given to only a few animals. Man is supposed to use his brain and not get caught in this predicament. We fought, I slashed and the wolf attacked.

He knocked me off balance. I reeled backwards, nearly overcome with fatigue. Fortunately he was unable to take advantage of this moment of truth and finish me off. He, too, was off balance and we both fell to the ground. I blinked and looked at him. He just sat there, his coal black eyes on me. It was almost as if a short truce was declared. We panted and stared at each other. Those eyes of his told the story. He was telling me that the fight had only begun. I swear the Devil was in those eyes; they were red with fire. Vengeance was there. I don't think we sat still for five seconds; the fight was on again.

In two steps he was in the air. This time I thought if I could control the head a little I had a chance to strike at the belly. He leapt with jaws open. I lifted my right forearm and made sure he caught it in his mouth. His force striking me knocked us to the ground and the knife was out of my hand. He tore rabidly at my sleeve. The smell of my blood gave him renewed energy. He was now in a feeding frenzy, as fierce as a shark's. I looked for the knife and tried to wiggle my way to it.

The wolf pulled me away from the knife time after time. He would release my arm just enough to try for the throat and I'd shield myself with the tattered parka. I felt the sharp fangs tearing into the sleeve, shredding it close to my flesh. His paws worked wildly at my chest and glanced blows off my face. It they connected they would slash my face to pieces. Nearly faint with exhaustion, and with what I figured was a final attempt, I lunged at the knife. I grabbed it and slashed at the snarling head locked onto my arm. There was a sudden release of the grip.

The wolf yelped as I struck flesh. He let go, backed off and ran about fifteen feet away. Blood came from the side of his face. He took a paw and rubbed the wound, then licked the paw. He whined and rubbed the wounded face in the snow. I crawled to the steps and pulled myself up. I lay there gasping the freezing air in; my lungs were on fire. The wolf looked at me and snarled again. I wasn't ready for the next round. I knew if he attacked it was over for me, yet he just stood there.

The first wolf hadn't died and all the while the fight was going on, he was dragging himself towards us, to join in as he was dying. A blood trail led from where I had stabbed him to the spot where the fight had taken place. He could have only served as a diversion, but it may have been enough. Not too far away, I heard the rest of the pack, calling as they came in on a dead run down the mountain.

I don't know where I got the energy to stand and open the cabin door and fall inside. I used my foot to *close the door and the latch fell home behind me. I was safe. I lay on the floor while the warmth of the cabin renewed my energy. I stood and heard a soft plop on the floor. The severed ear of the second wolf I had fought fell to the floor; it apparently had been caught in the sleeve of my parka.*

I stood for a moment, then fell on the bed. I lay there for who knows how long, maybe an hour or two. Finally I gathered myself, took the rifle off the pegs and looked out the window. The wolves were gone, blood was scattered over the ground. It belonged to me and the wolves. The dead wolf lay, a frozen carcass now. Slowly I opened the door a little and listened. Nothing. I saw no shadows in the trees. I thought they must have trotted off. I ventured onto the porch, looked around and waited for fifteen minutes. I knew their eyes were out there but I couldn't see them. The devils were waiting for another chance at me. I looked to the dock and saw nothing. I stared up the mountain trail and saw nothing. I decided I was going to show them what was in store for them if they returned. I went to the tool shed for two nails, hammer and block and tackle. On the big fir across from the cabin door, I threw the rope over a limb and hoisted the dead wolf up about six feet. I nailed the hind feet to the tree and let the head hang down. I knew they were watching but since I had the rifle, they weren't going to come out. I brought in more wood and several elk steaks out of the cooler shed and ate heartily after I cleaned up. The cheek wound wasn't as deep as I first thought.

Five days later Jack mentioned he hadn't seen anything more of the wolves. The traps were showing some promise. He wanted to go to the south pass to look for moose. Then later, on the 14th, he wrote a chilling account:

The Devil surely lives in these wolves. I went to the pass this morning and it nearly cost me my life. Today I found out this pack has only one aim, to kill me.

I rose before first light. It would take me all the daylight to go to the pass, wait an hour, then return. I filled two clips for the 30-06 and chambered another. Taking the canteen full of hot water and the binoculars, I started off. I stayed close to the shore line to avoid giving an open silhouette on the lake and moved quickly down to the south pass. I looked constantly across the lake and into the woods with the glass. I never saw anything.

I made good time and I arrived at the pass before mid-sun. I stayed out of sight behind the triangle rock. The animal trail was only a hundred yards off and from the vantage point, an easy shot. Nothing stirred except eagles. I thought they'd be further south now. After an hour I started back. I was getting cold and the hot water was gone, so I made a line back to the camp across the frozen lake. I wonder now if that choice led to the following event or if it would have occurred anyway.

Heading straight for the camp, I stopped several times and listened and looked with the glass. Not a sign of the wolves. I was over halfway back, about a mile to go. I thought I heard a rumble or something akin to it and I stopped. The only sound was of my own breathing. I guessed it was ice moving; it'll do that sometimes. I started again and went fifty yards and heard it again. When I stopped this time, it was barely audible but constant, not rising or lowering in volume. I heard something like it several years ago when a stampede of elk came by the south pass. I looked with the glass all around and didn't see anything yet. I hoped the ice wasn't breaking up, and

I began to walk faster.

The rumble changed and I stopped. It became louder. I looked again to the far side of the lake and saw snow being kicked up. I guessed it was a small avalanche at the mountain. I went half a mile and the rumble was now louder. It wasn't any avalanche. I put the glass on the far shore and saw black dots weaving back and forth. My breath had fallen on the lens and they fogged up a little, I couldn't make out what it was. Elk, I supposed. I cleared the lens and took another look. Wolves. Racing toward me as fast as they could travel. Perhaps there were thirty, all on a dead run. I could see the snow fly when they would hit deep drifts, but mostly between them and me it was pretty clear, because the wind had blown a lot of the snow off the ice. I removed my snowshoes and started to walk as quickly as I could. I knew if I broke into a run, the cold would get to me before the wolves. The distance was in my favor. I wanted to get back and make a stand and finally kill off as many as I could. Now it was personal.

I stopped again and they were looming nearer than I thought. I dropped the snowshoes and ran. Less than a half mile to the cabin and they were over a mile away. Fear of being shredded by the pack pushed me to the edge. I heard my heart pounding in my ears. I wondered if each pulse beat might be my last. The frozen air burned its way into my chest. The moisture in my lungs crystallized. I exhaled clouds of vapor. I said to myself, I'd be damned it they were going to kill me out here. I pushed on and the cabin was only a short distance ahead. I heard grunts and realized it was me. At last I saw the opening in the woods and the tiny dock signaling me to safe haven. The exhilaration of knowing that I was going to beat them made me start laughing. I touched the dry land and they were still a quarter mile off on the frozen lake. I ran to the cabin and stopped. I took the 30-06 off my shoulder, looked back to see the lead wolves about two hundred yards from the dock. Standing at the bottom of the steps I raised my rifle and aimed for the first round to be fired when they hit the land. I figured I could get two, maybe three, shots off before I had to retreat to the safety of the cabin. I looked down the barrel and saw the ferocious anger in the faces of the advancing beasts.

I heard, or thought I heard, a noise off to my right, and looked in time to see a wolf springing towards me off the porch roof.

The force of his landing sent me to the ground, and the vicious battle of a few days ago seemed to start all over again. His paw again slashed a line across my cheek. He knocked my rifle from me. It slid ten feet away, and he just stood there, eyes daring me to go for it. He didn't leap in attack as I thought he might, he just stood, issuing that low-pitched growl. I started to stand and while hunched over, I slowly backed toward the cabin porch. The wolf moved between me and the rifle. I felt the bottom step with my heel and figured I had just enough time to make it inside if I made one lunge for the door. I had nothing to lose.

The devil must have been able to read my mind. The others were now on the dry land and fifteen seconds from tearing me apart. I made one superhuman effort, knowing it might be my last. I jumped up and back as the lone wolf lunged. I hit the door and opened it as he landed on the porch and grasped my parka in his jaws. I shut the door as tight as I could and heard the others leaping onto the porch. The howling and growling sounded like a demons feasting around a caldron. I took the parka off and pulled as hard as I could, but in a sudden surge of power the wolf pulled the whole thing outside and the door slammed shut. I bolted it quickly. I had other parkas but the life I just saved was the only one I had. I heard the shredding of the parka and all around the cabin the savage howls continued.

If I could have only gotten that rifle inside, I would have found a way to finish off the whole pack then and there. I sat down and looked at my shaking hands. I suddenly realized I was very cold. Embers in the fireplace still glowed and I began to build a fire, a big fire. After an hour and many cups of hot coffee I began to thaw out. I walked to the front window and saw the one-eared wolf on his haunches watching the door. He turned his hate-filled eyes to meet mine. It was he that jumped me from the roof. I lay down on the bed and closed my eyes. Suddenly I realized I had a Colt .45 and several hundred rounds of ammunition in the foot locker.

The wolves stalked around on the porch, knocking the chairs off. Several times I heard them lunge at the door. It held strong. I heard several on the roof, pawing the snow away, looking for a way into the cabin. Several times I heard the sound of one losing its footing and sliding off with a thump. I felt like a trapped animal. Now the shoe was on the other foot, but I could reason and win.

I shouted obscenities at them and taunted them by tapping on the window. They all got quiet and looked at the door, thinking I was coming out. I laughed at their stupidity. I stood close to the high window pane and looked at Ol' One Ear. I tapped the pane again, and suddenly a wolf jumped up and we were face to face, save *the glass between us. I fired several rounds through the wall. I doubt if any made it outside. Again, I looked out the window and in the failing light I could only see that Ol' One-Ear was still there but the others were out of sight. Dare I open the door? Only a little? I chuckled; that's exactly what they wanted. They'd be in hiding and once the door was open, they'd lunge in and it would be all over. No, I was too smart for that. I hated them with all the hate I could muster and I got the feeling that it was mutual. It was now going to be a battle to the death, for them or me.*

The night settled in for the next fourteen hours. I cleaned the blood from my face and washed up. I was going to need all my strength for tomorrow's battle, for surely it was going to be final. I would hear an occasional noise outside, banging on the porch or a growl here and there. Tomorrow, it will be settled. Tomorrow.

This did not sound like the Jack Nelson I knew. He was such a good shot and so cool he was able to pick off any wolves that even gave him a shadow to look at. He did, however, show me once that he was human. He had changed, visibly and in personality, in 'Nam on November 10, 1967. We shared the same hut and he was going out almost every night on his patrol. He didn't report in daily to anyone. Sort of on his own. He'd go draw out his ammo in the evening and check what he hadn't used the next morning. Jack always had his sniper rifle with him.

Every morning he would come in, lay the rifle on the bed, then kneel down and pray. The morning I saw the change, he came in and put the rifle down like always. He knelt, folded his hands and threw up. He was crying and throwing up. I grabbed his helmet and put it under his chin. I got water and towels to clean him. He was a jumble of nerves, shaking so bad it was difficult to wash his face. He lay on the floor moaning. I said I was going for the medics. He grabbed me and made me swear that I'd never tell anyone, he'd be okay, he said, just give him a few minutes.

After I cleaned him up, we sat on the edge of my bed and chain-smoked several cigarettes. I left him for a few minutes while I bundled up his bedclothes and piled them next to the door. I wasn't going to push for answers, I knew they would come when he was ready to talk. His eyes were vacant and red. Jack was only twenty-two years old but he looked a hundred that morning.

We sat for another half hour smoking and I opened a bottle of Jack D and poured him some with water. In a few minutes, without emotion or waver in his voice, he said he had been in position and saw a target moving in the dark. He used night-vision goggles but the damn batteries were nearly dead. There was enough moonlight to see only indistinct shapes. This lone figure moved along the trail he'd been watching for several nights. The target was carrying a satchel charge in front of him. He knew a spot for the target to pass and set up for the shot. The target came into the sights and he fired. He had a good hit and sat there for another two hours before going to confirm the shot. When he got there, he discovered it was a pregnant girl who had been moving about in the night.

He looked at me and asked what the hell was wrong with this world. He stood, went and took a shower and we never spoke of it again. But he was never the same. He often said he dreamed that they were after him, but never defined who they were. He said he couldn't see them very good.

Now, in his cabin, I put my face in my hands. Bill went to the plane to call for an emergency relay on 121.9. He came back and said a Canadian Air Force plane heard it and relayed our situation to the home airport. They would have an ambulance waiting for us. Bill went outside again to have a look-see around the place. He took his .45 along.

I was almost afraid to read Jack's last entry. Maybe in these last few lines I could find what was about to take my friend's life. It began on January 15th:

I rose early, made a pot of coffee and sat in the dawning day, waiting to see what their move was going to be. It had been silent all night, except around 2 o'clock. I heard growling and snarling again, almost like they were fighting among themselves. There was a banging of something but I couldn't make it out. Even though the windows were high, I decided to board them up and thought I had enough boards leaning against the outside of the cabin to do it. The tool shed was a few yards away. If they were gone when it was light, I would try to get the place boarded up. Doing the work out back would put me in the most vulnerable position. I needed the rifle and the pistol at all times.

At the first light I saw Ol' One-Ear sitting out there still. I looked out all the windows and didn't see anything else. The rest were all gone. The fighting I'd heard must have been a squabble as to whether to stay or not. I had won this little victory so far. The rifle still lay out in the open. I knew the mechanism had frozen so I had to get to it first. I looked for a long time out the front windows. Nothing stirred. The lone sentry sat sniffing the air and watching the door. I rattled the door and his ears perked up. I listened for other sounds. There were none. I pulled the hammer back on the Colt and slowly opened the door. He watched me.

I braced my foot against the door, open only enough to see him. It was an awkward stance but I raised the Colt. In quick succession I fired off three rounds. Snow kicked up all around him and he ran off. I stepped onto the porch and fired in his direction. The .45 is a loud weapon. The sounds of the reports echoed back and forth across the lake. Suddenly realizing I was outside I looked around for a possible attack. There were no wolves to be seen. I started to laugh and couldn't help myself. I called out for them to come and fight. I shouted and cussed at them. My voice seemed not to travel beyond the nearby trees. I grabbed the rifle and put it in the cabin.

Quickly I went to the tool shed and got the hammer and nails. I grabbed long boards and threw them in the cabin and some more around back. I had the .45 out, hammer back all the time. Once in the back I put the .45 in my belt and as quickly as possible put up boards on the windows. I only wanted to prevent them from coming through the windows so I left some space to see out. I did the same for the side windows.

Walking to get the ones up front, I noticed that the door to the food locker was opened slightly. The peg had been knocked out of the hasp. I froze in place. I drew the .45 and slowly moved to the locker.

I listened at the door. The locker is about ten feet long and six feet wide with shelves for the food. I keep hooks in the roof for the meats to hang on. I had plenty of elk meat to last the winter. Slowly I opened the door and pointed the pistol inside. The sun hadn't risen enough to give much light, but I could see the elk meat was gone and canned goods strewn about. That was the noise last night, the devils taking the food. I swore at them and started to shut the door. Suddenly a ferocious sound came from within the locker. A wolf lunged at me, fangs exposed. Impulsively I leaned hard against the door and heard several others inside join in the charge. The wolf hit the door, but my weight was against it. Only a leg managed to make it through the opening and I pushed with all my strength. I heard the wolf's bone snap. The others kept leaping at the door. The broken leg prevented the hasp from making true. Leaning harder against the door, I took the Colt and fired at the leg until it fell to the ground and the door closed. I quickly put the peg in the hasp and ran into the cabin. The fight was back on. In the distance I heard others in the pack making their way back. Grabbing the boards, I nailed them to the windows from the inside.

By now the wolves were outside and howling, determined to get to me. They slammed against the door time after time. I fired the 30-06 through the door. Occasionally I would hear one of them yelp and looked to see it limp off. They began to hit the window in the back. They were on the roof, pawing and digging frantically at the timbers. The door was going to hold and I went to the window to see One-Ear sitting in his place of command. A window broke in the back, sending glass on the floor. I went back to see a board torn loose and I fired at a wolf through the broken window. I hit him solid. He went down and didn't move. Another took its place and jumped at the window where I stood. I could feel his hot breath through the opening. Again I fired and sent this one limping off.

I heard the front glass break and turned to see if I

could take some out there too. The door was still holding as they hurled themselves against it. I heard snarling and growling all over the cabin, on the ground and overhead. It seemed to be everywhere, all around me. I shouted and screamed at them, but that caused them to intensify the fight. I guess there were now twenty-five wolves now. They must have called in reinforcements, I laughed. Glass now flew into the cabin from another window and I saw the paws of the wolf inside the window, hanging on; the head popped up. Without aiming, I fired and hit him between the eyes, knocking him out of view.

Another window broke. I went to it and fired at the wolf trying to climb in. The loose board in the back was torn off and I heard another crash of glass. I turned to see the front half of a wolf through the window. I fired the Colt several times and the wolf fell limp into the cabin. Another took its place, I fired and it fell outside. I grabbed a board and quickly nailed it up. As soon as it was done, I heard the now too familiar sound of a wolf banging against it. I stood to the side and when I saw the wolf leap up, I shot and killed it. The animals' raging noise made me unaware of the sounds of my guns going off.

One wolf made a valiant lunge straight at the front window. He hit it full force, breaking the glass and sending pieces in my face. The blood ran down into my shirt as I reeled and fired. He hadn't made it in. I heard the boards in the back being pounded and turned to see a board knocked to the floor. Blood from the cut above my eyes ran down and blurred the vision in one eye. I saw a wolf come through the window opening. I fired and it fell at my feet. Another was on his way in and died hanging half in and out. The howling now grew to a fevered pitch. I grabbed the board and nailed it crosswise, *leaving the wolf hanging there to plug the hole.*

They continued to bang on the door. The hinges were beginning to loosen. There didn't seem to be any way of stopping this onslaught. They kept coming. I would kill them and more would take their place. I thought I had killed a hundred. I had to reload the clips for the Colt and that meant I had fired at least sixty rounds. The barrel of the 30-06 was hot from firing. Every once in a while when I looked out I would see One-Ear yelping encouragement to the others and I would take special aim at him, but he always managed to duck in time. I yelled in a rage at him to take a stand.

Once again I heard a board hit the floor and turned to see they had breached the side window. One wolf was in and died mid-leap. Another board hit the floor in the back and the dead wolf was pushed in by an advancing wolf. They smelled victory. They had two windows to come in and as fast as I'd kill one, another took its place. The wounded wolves in the cabin kept trying to get to me. I quickly counted six wolves at my feet and several were trying to get through the windows at the same time. They plugged it up themselves. I fired and one fell outside giving another a chance to get in. For only an instant it seemed to grow quiet.

I stopped and reloaded. I heard the growling and yelping of the call. With renewed effort, they attacked. They couldn't be this smart. What seemed like five or six hit the door at the same time that many or more came through the windows. The door gave way. I had the 30-06 in one hand and the Colt in the other. I fired wildly at them. It seemed hopeless now. They were pouring in the windows and through the door. I had figured I was going to die outside firing at them, not in here.

I lunged past the door through the fangs that tore at my pants legs. The vengeance was renewed as I went outside. I fired at everything that moved. The wolves were dying fast at this close range. The .45 slugs sent them reeling back, throwing them into the snow around the cabin. It looked as if I was making headway. They tore at my pants and had hold of the parka. Several jumped on my back, teeth clenched on the hood, whipping their heads back and forth. I almost lost balance several times but kept firing. This seemed to go on forever and ever. After ten rounds the 30-06 ran dry. I threw it to the ground and put my hand in my pocket to find the clip for the .45 when it ran dry.

The frenzy began to die a little and I felt that there might be a glimmer of hope for me. I still fired but they weren't attacking with the same ferocity. Their number was dwindling. I was exhausted. I didn't even realize that it was well below zero degrees outside. Suddenly as if there was a shout, they stopped the attack and ran for the nearest cover.

I fired wildly, changed the clip and kept firing. I stopped to hear the noise echo in the valley. They were gone. I had won. I ached all over. Blood was frozen to my face. They had made it though the parka and gashed my arm. The blood froze the sleeve to my arm, possibly keeping me from bleeding to death. I was so exhausted. I sat down in the middle of the dead wolves and slowly looked about while I gasped in icy air. I must have sat there for half an hour. Aching all over, I managed to stand and survey the scene. I counted twelve dead wolves outside in front. I went out back and saw six more. Inside the cabin there were eight. I loaded the 30-06 and the clips for the Colt

Slowly, with agonizing pain in my arm, I lugged the wolves from the cabin and piled them in front, about fifteen yards away. I took the ones from the back and piled them on top of the others. My arm was becoming numb. When I hauled the last one to the pile, I fell exhausted to the snow. I muttered, "Twenty-six of you died and you will be a monument to the rest." I dragged myself up and went to the tool shed. The red can was full.

Returning to the pile of wolves, I heavily doused them with the kerosene. I went back into the cabin, took a stick that was on fire and returned to the porch. I swung the torch in an arc and it landed at the bottom of the pile. The kerosene lit and the flames worked their way around and up the wolves. Soon the whole pile was afire. I had the .45 in my hand and half fell, half sat on the edge of the porch. The pain in the arm was getting worse. I was afraid to look at it. I stared at the Colt. The beautiful blue of the steel contrasted with the white snow in the sunlit background. I contemplated killing myself, denying the wolves of the pleasure. I quickly put this out of mind. It would have meant that they won. I knew they would be back. They must come back.

I stood and walked around the magnificent fire. The stench of burning hair and flesh, even though repulsive and horrible to smell, seemed to revive the prehistoric suppressed animal in me. It must lie lurking in all of mankind, hiding there until the events of life cause it to emerge in its ugly manifestation. I enjoyed it, every crackle of the fire; the smell filled my nostrils and I enjoyed watching the burning, the victory. I felt like the caveman winning over the saber-tooth tiger or other beast where survival was the name of the game. I enjoyed the scene. I let out a yell and shouted for One-Ear to return and let's

reignite the fight. I cursed the wolves and at the same
time lamented for them. They died in battle, a good fight
to be sure, but I had won. I stood there almost in reverie
and looked at the setting sun. The setting sun. I realized
the fight had gone on almost all day.

The sun began to move and I couldn't understand why.
It started to move in little circles, then bigger ones. The
fire danced before me, I could see wolves running over
the frozen lake. I saw them crashing through the locker
door and taking the elk. I saw them coming through the
windows and door. I slowly sank to the snow. Above the
flames was One-Ear looking at me, licking his chops, not
bearing his fangs but just standing there, watching me
die. I struggled to stand again but fell. The only sound I
heard was my gasping for air. I lay on my back not able to
move. Shadows played in the firelight. The wolves were
the ones dancing the victory dance. I could not move. I
lay there. I asked myself, is this the way Man dies? Did
the Neanderthal man die like this? Were we to return to
be the savage in order to win and live or to lose and die? I
don't know how time passed or if it did. The sky got gray
and then quickly black. I closed my eyes. In the distance
I heard a wolf howl.

I don't know how or why it happened. It must have
been hours later. I lay in the snow and I slowly became
conscious, only to feel a tongue licking the wound on my
face. I smelled the hot breath of a wolf over me, licking
the wound. I didn't move anything but I felt the Colt
still in my hand. I slowly raised it and as I did the wolf
let out a little whine. He began to lick harder and faster.
I knew it was close to tearing my flesh. I raised the Colt
and the wolf didn't know when I pulled the trigger and
sent the slug into its head. The force of the round threw

him backward off me.

I was wide awake now. I sat up and looked in the moonlight to the cabin. I crawled around the smoldering little pile that was once the bloodthirsty pack and onto the porch. I heard a wolf cry somewhere. I pulled myself up and went inside. I lit the lantern, nailed the windows securely with the boards. The fire was rekindled and soon sending out warmth. I heard a wolf give a mournful cry once again. He was alone. He was on the other side of the lake. He was far, far away.

I won. They won't bother me anymore. I won.

Jack Nelson had signed the last page. I looked over at the body. Bill and I walked back over to him, lowered the sheet and looked at his face. There were no scars. I slowly pulled the right sleeve up and saw a perfectly good arm. There were empty shell casings from the Colt scattered around the floor. Rifle casings were also strewn about. The window panes were intact.

We walked outside. There was no evidence of the fire he wrote of. We went to the food locker and, pulling the pin from the hasp, opened it to see several slabs of elk hanging from the hooks. We looked at each other and went back to the cabin. Tales of strange events always follow those who winter over in the desolate parts of the world.

One thing was sure. From the wild look on his face, something had happened. We all have the "they's" that we want to get away from. Some of us face them outright; some of us let them destroy us. Sometimes we find an even ground between truth and fantasy which we call sanity. That ground slipped away from Jack, I guess.

We wrapped the body in a blanket and gently carried

him to the plane. We eased him into the underbelly cargo hold and locked it. I went back to the cabin to get a few things of his.

I got the Colt and the 30-06, then picked up the notebook to take along too. Under the back cover was the lone gray ear of a wolf.

We taxied out and took off, passing the campsite as we lifted off. I'd almost swear a wolf stood at the end of the dock, watching us depart.

Night Flight

Headlights stabbed into the night, barely penetrating the murky darkness. The car raced up the winding road, made narrower by the oak trees bending their huge limbs down, trying to grab the passerby. Unseen dust flew up as darkness quickly filled the vacuum behind the speeding vehicle. On a distant high crag was the reason the car sped in the night.

There at the imposing structure, two figures dressed in dark clothes darted among the shadows. They needed the important cover of darkness to execute their plan. The entry door squeaked at the Olson Observatory when the pair slipped inside. A dim bulb at the far end of the hallway illuminated the pale walls. Red exit lights vied for attention. One of the figures turned and inserted an iron bar through the handle of the door, preventing it from being opened.

No words were spoken, even though they felt they were alone. They acted quickly; their pursuer wasn't far behind them in their race against time. The man opened another door leading to the huge domed room housing the telescope. He cautiously searched for signs of movement and held his breath, listening for telltale sounds that they weren't alone. After he stepped inside, the woman followed. Silent footfalls sent them into the large open space below the dome, soft echoes ricocheting off the smooth walls.

Red lights blinked on the telescope and on control panels against the walls. The man and woman looked at each other. Their eyes, now accustomed to the scant light, allowed them to navigate in the cavernous room. He nodded to her and she smiled back.

He dropped his backpack, and large strides took him to the control panel marked Dome. Relays clicking into action interrupted the silence, sending voltage to motors operating the curved doors overhead. Dropping her own backpack, the woman unzipped small pouches and removed equipment. The doors moved to full open quickly and quietly as they prepared for the dangerous departure.

"Emile must not be far behind. I hear his automobile." Her accent betrayed her Eastern European origins.

"We still have time." He helped her slip on the parachute and snapped another harness to rings that held the shroud-lines on either side of her shoulder. "Get into position under the opening." He looked up and helped position her.

Once in place, she stood still, looked to the floor and took in a deep breath, while he unwound the lines of the second harness. The Mylar balloon in the center of the coil crackled as the nylon lines were rolled off. These lines were laid in a spiral path encompassing her in the middle. That done, he snapped the helium filler tube to the Mylar balloon. In a smooth motion he uncoiled the flexible plastic tubing and clicked it home in the helium bottle's fitting. He opened the valve and all was set. The helium made a welcoming hiss as it began to fill the balloon.

He stopped and looked at her. Fresh air slipped across the dome's rim and filled the room, cooling his neck where sweat trickled down to his collar. They heard the car stop in the parking lot and a door slam shut. They figured Emile would take about ten minutes to get inside.

He put his hands on her shoulders and gave her a gentle kiss, hoping that he would be able to control his emotions. Her hair was bound tight against her head, a far cry from the flowing black locks that first attracted him. She wasn't a stunning beauty but carried herself in a manner that captured his attention, and ultimately they had blended into lovers.

Events over the past five months had thrown them together, locking them in a battle with teams from several countries. The government needed important information and, along with Emile, he and she made up a team to secure the secret documents. Each member alone

was to obtain just one third of it. Once combined into a package, if it fell into the wrong hands, the information could cause years of hostile international relations to follow.

A week earlier she had told him that she was able to get all three pieces of information and had secured a third-party buyer. She begged him to come with her. His devotion to his country was tested by his love for her. He told her she should go this night; he promised to follow once she was hidden in another country and able to contact him. It would be easier for everyone this way. She had agreed and told him of the entire plan, including the helium balloon escape and using a sport parachute to fly to the waiting submarine.

There was a loud clang at the door, dissolving the kiss. They both looked to the door, hoping it was still secure. She looked up at him and he enveloped her in his arms. They held each other tightly as they kissed again. Her warm mouth sent intense feelings charging through him. He knew it was foolish to wait any longer.

He held her back and looked at the filmy plastic as it expanded. They whispered their love for each other.

"Let me check the harnesses again." His hands moved expertly over the parachute and harness leading to the rising envelope of helium. He stepped back, watching the envelope rise past the lip of the open dome and into the clear night air.

No surface wind stirred, but once aloft, she would drift gently out to sea and the safe pick-up by the submarine. After radio contact with the submarine, she'd send a signaling light to them. When they responded likewise to show their position, the balloon would be released. After a ten-second free-fall, she'd open the steerable parachute and glide to the submarine.

Repeated crashing sounds came from the outside door, then silence. Emile was seeking another way in. The balloon's lines, now off the floor, tightened against her weight. He rushed up to her and gave her a quick kiss and watched her drift up from his touch, into the star-filled night.

He sprinted to the control panel and shut the dome doors. The relays clicked again and the smooth operating doors closed. He walked to the front door and removed the iron bar.

Out in the parking lot he went to his car and removed the night vision goggles along with a pair of binoculars. He made his way to the edge of the cliffside observatory's foundation and leaned against the railing. Emile came up beside him and they both watched the pale silver balloon sail over the ocean, becoming smaller and smaller all the time, as she rose to the desired 4,000 feet.

The men stood in silence, looking through the wispy green light at the star-lit balloon. After six minutes there was the bright signal light followed shortly by two flashes. The signal to drop and fly to the submarine. They couldn't see her, only the filmy silver teardrop suddenly shooting up, indicating she had released.

"Were you successful?" Emile lowered his glasses and turned off the light amplifying goggles.

He sounded almost remorseful, "Yes, I disconnected the ripcord."

Pirate's Gold in Fernandina

I stood on the seawall as waves thrust against the rocks, creating a cold, penetrating spray. Fierce northeast winds pelted my face with near-frozen droplets. I gazed at the horizon, almost obscured by the fading light, hoping to get a glimpse of a light or see a silhouette against the rough ocean. If I did see a light, it could be one of a hundred shrimp boats or cargo ships that plied these waters off Fernandina Beach.

I couldn't believe I was there, against reason, looking for a light that would indicate the location of a lunatic frantically trying to raise a Spanish treasure chest full of gold. Again and again the spray brought me to my senses, which told me to go home to a warm fire and a glass of wine. It was three nights ago that I heard the story, which I really knew was a tale that spreads around fishing villages like this to stimulate the imagination of visitors. Yet, there I stood.

Three days earlier, I sat at the foot of Centre Street watching the sunset across the Amelia River when a man approached, dropped a sea bag and sat on the opposite end of the long bench. He lit a cigarette, leaned back and inhaled deeply, seemingly to enjoy the extra nail in his coffin. The smoke blew my way as did the odor of an unwashed body.

"Beautiful sunset," he said, then coughed a few times before he spat in the water.

"Yeah, I come here when I think it will be nice," I replied, being civil but not looking at him, not wanting to engage in a conversation.

"I won't see many more of 'em," he said. I wondered if he was leaving town or dying of lung cancer. He continued, "Leaving town, headin' to Colorado."

"That's a beautiful state." I still did not want conversation.

He cut an eye towards me. "Believe in ghosts?" The question caught me off guard.

I looked at him. The stubbled beard had flecks of gray that matched the hair showing from underneath his watch cap. The well-worn jeans and heavy coat would help keep off the cold night air. "No, can't say that I do."

Without questioning my answer, he continued. "A year ago I worked on the shrimper Loosiana. Captain was mostly crazy, but we made some good hauls. He liked to drink away his profits, though. From what I heard he was real in debt. After one night of pickling his liver over his losses and staggering home, he met a stranger. This stranger told him a tale about a sunken Spanish galleon just off shore that held a lot of gold. It was a galleon captured by the pirate Luis Aury.

"The captain was desperate and took the bait. He told us this the next day and instead of heading out to haul shrimp, we went to the spot where the stranger said the treasure was. Me and the other mate thought he was crazy but went along for the fun of it and it wasn't going to be as much work as before." He paused and took a long drag off the cigarette and watched the last rim of the sun slip behind the distant trees.

A heavy northeast wind blew in and the seas got rough real quick. We tried a lot to get the captain to head back but he was drunk and kept dragging the bottom. In a pitching sea like that, the lines go slack and then taut a lot. But one time they got taut and didn't slack up. We pulled in the net and as we did the wind kicked up worse. The seas were close to ten feet. Would you believe it, there was a box in the net. Looked real to me an' the captain was laughing like a madman. We began to swing the net on board when the net gave way and the box hit the water." The snap of his fingers startled me. "Disappeared that quick." He sat back and looked at a fingernail in the twilight, and again cut an eye toward me. I began to enjoy this fish tale.

"Captain wanted to stay, but Reggie and me was scared and got on the radio and hailed another shrimp boat heading to the jetties. The captain said if we told anyone he would kill us -- he'd a done it too. The other boat came alongside and we boarded her – all but the captain. The last we saw of the *Loosiana* she was riding low with waves crashing over her."

"Did he make it back?" I asked as if I believed him.

"No, but nights when the ocean's rough, you can see a green light just south of the jetties, 'bout two miles out."

"Why are you telling me this?"

"Well, I'm leaving, Reggie died two months ago and we thought someone here should know the story, just in case the light is seen and no one can explain it. We sorta felt we at least owed that to the captain."

"Two miles out, huh?"

"Yep, go to Main Beach and stand where you can line up the first palm tree from the parking lot and there's a big rock at the seawall with a black spot on the top. Line both of them up and about two miles out you'll see the green glow of the *Loosiana*."

He got up and abruptly left after shouldering the sea bag. He didn't turn around but gave a little wave with the hand that held another cigarette.

So, here I stand in the cold gale force winds, wet with the spray and, like a fool, half hoping the story was true. A few people came by and must have wondered why I was standing there but I wasn't about to tell them. Lightning flashed on the ocean horizon several times and I figured this story was a good one, given the stormy night.

I returned to my car and had to loop the parking lot to leave. I gave one last look and almost wrecked the car. I thought I saw a green flash in the distance. I told myself it was reflections of the nearby lights. I parked the car and returned to the designated spot.

The hair on my neck stood up and I didn't even feel the cold spray this time. There was the green light on the ocean. It flickered as if on a boat riding rough waters from crest to crest. It was not a pinpoint of light but more like a green glowing ember.

Believe me or not, I don't care. But it happened and I saw it. Listen, as the next nor'easter gathers strength, go out to Main Beach and see for yourself.

Go ahead, you'll see.